WATTLE & DAUB

WATTLE
& DAUB

BRIAN COUGHLAN

etruscan press

Etruscan Press
Wilkes University
84 West South Street
Wilkes-Barre, PA 18766
(570) 408-4546

 Wilkes
University

www.etruscanpress.org

Published 2018 by Etruscan Press
Printed in the United States of America
Cover design by Lisa Reynolds
Interior design and typesetting by Julianne Popovec
The text of this book is set in Baskerville

First Edition

17 18 19 20 5 4 3 2 1

Library of Congress Cataloguing-in-Publication Data

Names: Coughlan, Brian, 1977- author.
Title: Wattle & daub / Brian Coughlan.
Description: First edition. | Wilkes-Barre, PA : Etruscan Press, 2018.
Identifiers: LCCN 2017049279| ISBN 9780998750835 | ISBN 9780998750859
Subjects: | GSAFD: Short stories.
Classification: LCC PR6103.O91 A6 2018 | DDC 823/.92--dc23
LC record available at https://lccn.loc.gov/2017049279

Please turn to the back of this book for a list of the sustaining funders of Etruscan Press.

To Ciara & Jim

WATTLE & DAUB

A Nuisance 3
Prologue 11
Re-union 21
The Equator 31
The Witness 41
Enhanced Forgiveness 49
Gnawing Fear 59
Human Butterfly 67
Malingerer 77
Abattoir 87
Creator 99
Downhill 109
Crusader 119
Standard Operating Procedure 129
Widow Maker 139
The Accursed 149
Interview with a Campfire 159
Tinkerman 169
Human Resources 179
Altar Boy 191
Ill Conceived 201
F-unfair 211

Portions of this work have appeared in the following:

'Abattoir' appeared in *The Galway Review*
'A Nuisance' appeared in *Thrice Publishing Anthology August 2016*
'Downhill' appeared in *Lunaris Review* and in *Unthology 10* as
    'One for the Ditch'
'Standard Operating Procedure' appeared in *Litbreak Magazine*
'Re-Union' appeared in *Fictive Dream*
'Malingerer' appeared in *Storgy* and *The Legendary*
'Enhanced Forgiveness' appeared in *Toasted Cheese Literary Journal*
'The Equator' appeared in *Crack the Spine Literary Magazine* and in
    The Blotter Magazine
'Human Resources' appeared in *Sentinel Literary Quarterly*
'Creator' appeared in *ChangeSeven Magazine*
'Tinkerman' appeared in *Bitterzoet Magazine*
'Interview with a Campfire' appeared in *The Bohemyth*
'The Witness' appeared in *Litro NY*
'Gnawing Fear' appeared in *The Exceptional Writer Literary Magazine*
'Widow Maker' appeared in *The Ham Free Press*

WATTLE & DAUB

A NUISANCE

No longer pubescent. A long, bare neck exposed, lips painted vermillion, hips pushed out to one side in the full-length mirror. As an adult, she stands unsmiling, gooseflesh risen, toes frozen, in a pair of open-toed sandals, covered in the feathers of her new disguise. The mobile phone lightly dings with another link in the chain of messages. Her dress, pulled from the wreckage of the boxes, wrinkled to all hell, is smoothed-out using both hands. All the sinews in her neck strain. Red raw knuckled hands. Bony protuberant knees, on long white spindly legs. Unsmiling, dimpled cheeks assess the overall effect. In the silence, every sound of planned escape is amplified: the sound of elastic straps snapping, scream of bristles running through hair, shriek of wheezing lungs. A buried clock ticks from somewhere in the tower of boxes. Still too soon – she lies back down on the old bed.

A little earlier she'd dozed off, despite the hard glare from a bed-side lamp, despite the greasy smell from the pillow, despite the damp-ness of antiquated sheets. Her dream so shockingly-deliciously vivid that with a shudder of disgust the pillow slips from her grasp, and with the fluttering of eyelash she awakens and for one horrible moment does not know where she is. It's only in the repeated blink of her upward fac-ing eye that there's a gradual returning recognition, via the unpleasant smell of damp. Surrounded by shadows from the tower of boxes, deep in the middle of nowhere, the room at the end of the hallway, a room full of boxes: filled with clothes, tins of food, mildewing books, toiletries, old magazines, broken shoes; her entire life's junk boxed-up, piled-up, and listing.

Now she needs a glass of water, her throat burning – except they don't have glasses in this house: instead you make do with a cup. They have so many different kinds of cups, from multiple unrelated sets. None of them match. You ask for a glass and they roll their eyes. "What's wrong with a cup? It's the same thing. Isn't it?" Long winding hallway through this unfamiliar house to the kitchen, with cold floor-tiles all the way. Pitch black, the light switches being impossible to find; she has to feel her way along the walls, like a blind person, turn the corner, go past the phone in its alcove and there should be a door right there, and behind the door is a picture of the Last Supper and next to that picture she knows there is a light switch.

As she noisily fills her cup under the tap, lights go on in the hall-way. Her grandfather calls out: "Who's out there?" A pause and then he remembers, "Is that you Caroline?" He shuffles down the hallway, stops to watch from the doorway as she puts the cup to her mouth and takes a long drink of the ice cold water. "Sorry, I didn't mean to wake you," she whispers. He nods, still silhouetted, impatient for her to go back to bed. She shuffles past with her adulthood concealed beneath a long black dressing gown. He closes the kitchen door tightly behind her, to keep the heat in, and follows her. There in the hallway she experiences a sudden urge, to turn and give the old man a hug, but sensing her urge and fearing it, fearing the power of her frenzied youthfulness, he backs away quickly, retreats down the hall, wordlessly. "Night, then," she whispers, to herself.

In the box room she checks her phone: still charging. Sixty-three-percent charged; it's plugged into a loose wall socket. She thinks, composes a brief text message and presses send, then gets back under the damp covers leaving the bedside lamp on: she's used to housing-estate street-lights, not the absolute darkness of night-time in the middle of nowhere. And not just the box-room, but the whole ancient house, is alive again with the crackle of silence, a static wall amplified by night-fall. Tonight though is different; there is an additional low buzzing noise from one corner of the room, which is revealed as a large bluebottle – an angry bluebottle colliding with walls and curtains, circling above her, coming and going from the tower of boxes. While he appears angry, in truth he is madly, truly and irritatingly, in love with her. He circles her then dive-bombs towards those two pursed, kissable lips.

The duvet-cover resplendent with faded flowers and grinning ted-dy bears is retracted from long, thin legs while the bedside lampshade holds him hostage (he ricochets around the bulb and then spins out of control). Now out of bed she lumbers after him, armed with a magazine, as he tickles and tricks and dodges every attempt to smash his brains out. "I guess you're too smart for me," she says, as she tries to usher the bluebottle outside by opening a window. It'll surely leave of its own accord, she tells herself as ice cold air streams into the room: but the bluebottle refuses to leave, and why would he leave? He wants to be with her. Instead he runs along the walls, underneath the ceiling, calling her name in a plangent cry of love. Naturally she doesn't hear it that way, to her it sounds like angry buzzing.

"Well – have it your way then," she cries, now unwilling to con-cede defeat. Rolling up the magazine into a tube she chases him around the room. Their ballet of death is but a waste of time: when she stops to get her breath back so does he, and this continues from one dance to the next. After a lengthy re-think of strategy she tries to surprise him by sud-denly pouncing with a swing of the magazine and a cry of "Hiyaaah!" The bluebottle is already in the air by the time the glossy cover beats against the wall. Now he's in the curtains, hiding deep within labyrin-thine folds. She creeps towards them. Silent pantomime steps of exag-geration. She thinks she can see him, gleefully rubbing his feet together; she holds her breath, careful not to alert him, raises the magazine over her shoulder. Wait for it. Wait for it. Now! She swings her magazine at the curtain folds, cries-out in surprise as dust from her swipe engulfs her eyes, nostrils and mouth. "Atchoo!" she sneezes, again and again, until the dust is cleared out of her nose.

All this time a silhouette has been watching her from the doorway, watching Caroline prowl with eyes darting from one brief cameo of shadow to the next, phantom movements, waiting somewhere, on the carpet or under the bed, back in the folds of the curtain? "What are you doing out of bed?" it asks, pointedly. Catches her off-guard. Caroline stammers, tells her grandmother about the bluebottle. "Just ignore it and get back into the bed," scolds the old woman. This is no way to be carrying-on in the middle of the night. With no recourse to a fair trial the girl nods her head meekly, accepts the scolding voice, returns to the land of faded flowers and prancing teddy-bears and is tucked-in by the rough hands of her hard-breathing grandmother. The bedside lamp too, is switched off, the door closed firmly behind the retreating, muttering figure.

As soon as her grandmother is gone the bluebottle starts buzzing around the room again. What if she ignores it? What if she tells herself that it does not exist, will it stop then? When you ignore a problem it goes away by itself. That doesn't sound right. Then she feels a little tickle on the end of her nose, and there it is again, but along the top of her lip. She quickly switches on the lamp. Leaping from the bed of ponies and pixies she picks up her pillow, chases the bluebottle all over the bedroom again. All thoughtfulness and strategy is replaced by savagery. She swings and knocks over the lamp, throws the room into high shadows. With an unrelenting passion she chases the bluebottle out of the room and slams the door after it with a triumphant finality. Bereft, the bluebottle floats along the corridor, enters the other bedroom through a door left slightly ajar and becomes a silent stuck-to-the-wall witness.

In the other bedroom grandmother grunts; constantly, involuntarily, from the back of the throat. It comes, regardless of circumstance, like an indicator of life-force. "…and what would you have us do with her, huh?" she says, disrobing in countless little movements and all the time with her *huh-huh-huh* in the background. Her husband lies there with his back to her. "She should be with her father," he shouts. "Tell me something I don't know!" she hisses, as she stumbles towards the hook on the back of the door with her dressing gown held up in offering to the God of hooks. "She can't stay here, we know that much," and she climbs into the bed, pulling over the covers, slowly, slowly and with the very great ceremony that trivial tasks assume in the midst of crisis. "I'll never get to sleep now," cries the old man, his voice muffled by the pillow in his mouth.

It's a cold night; this is a cold house. Within a matter of minutes they are both asleep. Though it is only ten o'clock at night they are already well past a bed-time that has been strictly adhered to for as long as they can remember. Their dreams are unrecorded. The old man's mouth hangs open like a black-hole of nothingness, the old woman continues to vibrate in her sleep, now with a slower, more purposeful sounding *hung...hung...hung...* issuing from somewhere deep in the depths of her being.

When the girl's phone dings again it's time to go. Seventy-six-percent charged; that'll do. She pulls the plug from the socket, winds the cord in and round the prongs, and puts it in her bag. There are other things she needs from the boxes but they are too heavy to take down all by herself: things she'd like, but will have to do without. The few things she must bring: hairbrush, make-up bag, underwear, pyjamas, her good shoes that she hasn't had a chance to wear yet, earrings, her purse; they were all rescued from the boxes earlier, are all packed into a bag that goes on her back. Despite the cold she refuses to wear her coat, she wants to look good, to show off her figure to the man coming to collect her. And so, holding her shoes, she ghosts up the hallway and silently lets herself out of the house by a key still stuck in the lock.

It's dark outside but she isn't afraid. The flash-light will guide her way along the boreen to where it joins the main road. The beam of her torch is enough to follow, and when a car pulls up alongside her the silhouette behind the wheel is friendly. He taps the passenger seat, tells her to jump on in. Finally they meet. There is a fly in the car. It keeps smashing itself against the underside of the windshield. As they pull away she asks if she can let it out. The driver says ok, he lowers the electric windows. "You look different from your photo," she tells him. Apparently that doesn't matter, except that it does. His hand strays from the gear-stick to her frozen knee. "You're so cold," he says, innocently as the calloused palm of a hand with thick dark hair growing all around the knuckles tickles her knee and it's too warm in the car so that she can smell his cologne and underneath that his musk, a nasty stink. The radio comes on; it's too loud to hear anything, too loud to think straight. He crushes the bluebottle against the wind-shield. A little red squish mark on the glass.

"Stop for a minute," she asks him and he pretends not to hear her. How fast they are spinning through the night in this long black piece of metal and light brown leather interior. "I'm going to be car-sick!" she says, holding her mouth with a cupped hand and the thought of it going on his leather seats forces the wheels to come to a sudden screeching halt. He opens the lock on her door and she leaps out and is over a ditch before he can stop her. He will not follow her through the fields, he has no stomach for it, those hairy hands and that big round head. She's moving now through the darkness, her feet slither in the muck and if she feels hot breath on her face and the smell of bad breath it will be from a horse or a cow not from some smelly old creep. The bed-side lamp left burning will guide her back, back to that cold little room filled with boxes.

PROLOGUE

The bivouac of ripped tarpaulin, keeping the two pipes free from water, threatened to fall over; then did. In the same gale force wind and driving rain a banner that read "UNDERGROUND ENDURANCE TEST" billowed angrily. A team of helpers hurriedly rebuilt the bivouac under the adjudicator's instructions. To his tired mind the pipe endings looked like a pair of nostrils belonging to some buried behemoth; when in actual fact – there was a living, breathing man, lying in a coffin buried, under that pile of muck who was hoping to break the current world record, held by the Swede – Karlsson – who'd managed ninety-nine hours.

The adjudicator's concerns that safety measures as part of this world record attempt were ill-conceived and shoddily executed had not dissipated. There had been no communication with the man in the coffin for the last hour. If they dug him up now the attempt would end in agonising failure. If he didn't order that the man be dug up, and say if something had happened, like if the pipe was obstructed, it would be on his head. Naturally the adjudicator felt himself buried under the pressure and expectation of both the organisers and spectators. They had promised him high quality walkie-talkies. So where were they? What he was given was more like a solid plastic brick that worked only when inclined to do so.

Buried the regulation six-feet deep, in an over-sized coffin, Tim felt perfectly fine and dandy. He had a flashlight and a few books with him in case he got bored, but was instead, endlessly re-writing his story for the papers; imagining the possibility of a biography that a complete stranger, who claimed to be a writer, had suggested they write together. Turning off the flashlight to preserve the last set of batteries he arranged the details to fit snugly together into a story that could perhaps form the prologue; the writer had explained the notion of a prologue to him. It should begin so dramatically as to instantly suck the reader into his story.

It begins with his ship docked in Copenhagen. Leave out the bit about the *Blue Goose* nightclub and the drinking. Instead for some (as yet unspecified) reason he misses the curfew. As is the case for anyone who misses curfew he has to find somewhere else to sleep for the night. The doorway he has collapsed against seems as good to his drink-addled brain as anywhere else. When he wakes up later that night the temperature has dropped well below zero. It feels as if his bones have turned to ice. If he stays where he is the chances are he'll die of hypothermia. So he makes a racket, banging on the nearest door using the nearest heavy knocker (shaped like an iron fist), until finally lights come on and his hysterical pleading is rewarded by the door opening by degrees – revealing a candle-holding middle-aged man sporting an enormous handle-bar moustache.

Luckily for Tim the man who opens the door – Oswald, is an exceptionally kind and compassionate individual. Despite the smell of drink off Tim's breath and the no doubt dishevelled appearance of what might have been a tramp – Oswald ushers him inside his home and puts him sitting on a stool by the range with a rough blanket over his shoulders. 'Drink this' motions Oswald, putting the bowl to his lips. Tim drinks, scalding his throat with the first mouthful, blowing on subsequent mouthfuls of the delicious thick soup with a tongue burnt to a crisp.

Having recovered his senses sufficiently to throw his eye around the room it becomes clear that he's in a coffin maker's work-room. Certain things made this obvious: hammers, saws, the many half-finished coffins. Then trouble arrives in a pink dressing-gown and matching pink face-pack. When she sees there is a stranger in the work-room she puts her hand to her mouth and murmurs "Oswald – Oswald..." and then a string of fast unintelligible words that are in another language but yet betray their meaning with little effort, as far as the dishevelled Irishman is concerned.

The kindly man and his wife hold a whispered argument in the hallway while Tim licks the bowl clean. After a few minutes the coffin maker returns with a resolution. In broken English he explains that his wife is none too keen on Tim staying the night. Tim nods and instantly leaps to his feet. The bowl which had been buried in his lap falls on the ground, cracks in half, and the spoon which had rested so peacefully up until then is sent spinning across the floor. Oswald shakes his head and bids him sit back down again until he explains in full the scenario.

There is a compromise solution: if Tim is prepared to spend the night in the workroom he can stay – but the workroom door has to be locked, that is to say Tim would have to agree to being locked into the room until morning (all this by hand-signals and enactment). Tim nods his head and gives a thumbs-up sign to his new friend. Oswald shakes his hand and leaves him with the remainder of the candle. When the door closes Tim hears the key turning in the lock. Only then does he think: why did I allow myself to be locked up in a stranger's workshop?

Alone in the room with only the flickering light of the candle to guide him, he cautiously approaches the work bench. Not wanting to wake up his hosts or give away his intentions, he moves with timorous steps, halting – listening; shuffling forward a few more steps; halting – listening; until he is very close to a half-finished model whereupon he fails to notice the spoon and kicking it across the floor he winces as it ricochets off the skirting board, spins in the air briefly and then clatters all over the floor in an appalling manner. He listens; the flickering light of the candle provokes grotesque shadows in the room to skirt along the walls.

He examines the objects in the room; the tongue and groove slats; the hanging tools covered in a thin film of wood dust; the vice, silently gripping two pieces of the base together; the stained cans of lacquer and the overpowering smell of the wood glue is so powerful a stimulant it causes Tim's head to throb as he wanders from one corner to another. Oswald keeps his workroom so neat and tidy. It pleases Tim enormously, but all of Oswald's tools hanging from the walls and all of his works in progress are nothing but distractions from the finished article, lying on two trestles at the back of the room.

A thing of beauty. The open top reveals cream silk, tufted and pleated immaculately and set-off by the dark high gloss finish of the wood. Catching hold of the metal swing handle nearest him he breathes deeply the intermingling aromas of wood glue, upholstery, lacquer and simple pine. With the pillow under his head cradling him delicately and the satin pleating enveloping him in a warm embrace he discovers the coffin to be extremely comfortable. It is heavenly to lie back in the coffin, surrounded by all that beautiful warm padding. To make it even cosier still he reaches for the lid and pulls it over the top, leaving the least little gap for air to get in. Happily, contentedly, he sleeps that way until morning when he's woken by the screaming of Oswald's wife – who has discovered him – after Oswald had declared the visitor to have inexplicably disappeared from a locked and windowless room!

* * *

Just over ninety-nine hours earlier the sound of the earth and stones hitting off the lid of the coffin as they buried him produced a giggle of delight and the looming excitement of breaking an obscure world record; his name spreading from this dark place to every corner of the globe; going down in history. In the town they had mocked him and many said he would only be able to stick it for an hour or two, at most. He knew differently of course. All he had to do was stay where he was and bide his time, which he had, for all those black silent hours, while the same story swirled around and around in his head, for the prologue.

And he was not alone; Cyril the spider, as Tim had christened him, was back again. Having explored the hilly regions of Tim's inner thighs and gone as high up as the alpine region of his raised kneecaps, the spider was now returning to sea-level. Tim's face contorted and frozen in an open-mouthed expression gazed fixedly on the swirl of a wood knot on the underside of the lid, inches from the tip of his nose. The blood now draining from his cheeks robbed them of their usual purplish flush and all at once a thin line of drool formed in the corner of his down-turned mouth and dripped in anguish with a barely perceptible tap on the pillow under his head. The spider traversed the folds of his shirt, circumnavigated his high collar and followed the steep curve of the neck so that it could crawl around the eyes, examine the nostril caves and finally scamper abruptly into the wide open black hole of mouth.

Six feet, give-or-take, above him, the adjudicator – having checked his official time piece – nods his head emphatically, and immediately two grave-diggers attack the soil with a cheer rising up from a crowd of thousands that has gathered around, and includes members of a local marching band nervously tuning up their instruments. Scratching sounds work their way toward him through the heavy earth, as huffing and puffing, the two men work their shovels and quickly begin to form a pile of soil on either side of the grave.

Expectant faces watch the men work while the rain doubles in fury and the adjudicator feels his socks (absolutely sapping) inside his boots. Best not to think about it, he says softly to nobody but himself. He pretends to be of the same mood as the crowd as he watches through a haze of rising steam the swinging shoulders, the bowing heads, the delicate slow-motion movement of the shovels through the air when transporting away earth and then the sudden vicious scooping sound as the shovels stick into the ground, pushing down and back slowly passing through the air, again with more dirt.

As if to provide some welcome light entertainment to the crowd, a small boy, wrapped in an enormous puffy jacket and sporting a woollen hat, breaks free from his mother and walks bow-legged and unsteady towards the grave; sadly his bid for freedom is disappointed by her long reach and so there are tears and a red face scrunched up into an angry ball as he is escorted back to his cell: a waiting buggy, where he is strapped and bolted-in securely.

"Tim, Tim we're nearly there boy!" shouts one of the men digging.

Buried in the still silent earth, his mind plays tricks, begets endings; in one of them, pressed for time, Oswald and his wife are furiously dressing and readying him for display. She removes a palate and applies make-up over his face and all the way up around his crow's nest. She paints his lips decisively a bright livid pink. Oswald working on his suit, pulls and preens every inch of jacket, shirt, straightens his tie, his trousers, so that he will look natural; places the stiff hands one on top of the other, wrapping the rosary beads around his interlocking fingers. But on this occasion they don't have time to smile at each other in recognition of the fine work; already the screws in the lid are being undone and the drummer in the band has broken into a little drum-roll.

The lid of the coffin is removed carefully. The chalkboard by the side of the grave tells everyone that he has broken the record by just 1 hour. As the lid is removed, a television camera cranes over the bent back of one of the digger men – and there is Tim lying supine in his coffin, wearing a pair of dark shades to protect his eyes from the light. At first there is no movement from him. The adjudicator shouts at everyone to stand well back and give him some air. Is he or isn't he? There is a moment. Silence. Only the sound of a crow cawing from a nearby tree.

Tim finally gives a double thumbs-up to the camera. A television reporter scrambles past security down into the hole for an exclusive interview amidst the screams and cheers of the assembled crowd.

"Did the feeling of claustrophobia bother him?"

"No, not a bit," replies Tim.

"What were you thinking about all that time?"

"My schooldays, time in the navy, and the like," answers the new world record holder as he allows them to dress him in a warm woollen jumper.

* * *

He didn't get to use his prologue. The proposed biography never materialized. By way of epilogue – he was the World Record Holder for just three weeks. Then a man named Chavez in Venezuela went nine hours longer. After Chavez, the Swede, Karlsson had another crack at it; he suffocated when the back-fill crushed his air pipes. Then a chap in Chile went ten hours longer than the Venezuelan but was subsequently accused of cheating (sketchy details). The local priest denounced any further live burial attempts by Tim as "grossly macabre" and vigorously objected every time a re-staging was brought up. And after that the world, collectively speaking, lost interest in the live burial world record, and it died a death.

RE-UNION

'm prone to rather severe bouts of sleep apnoea, with associated choking. Which might go some way towards explaining why I was the very last person in our household to be woken by the sound of our continuously ringing doorbell; depressed by an unknown finger – producing one so very long high-pitched ding but no dong. With no other reason than to provide an accompanying heavy back-beat, our recently acquired antique brass knocker began smashing, repeatedly, against its plaque. Our two small children were already in the room, crying, trembling, stuck to each other, utterly traumatised – although I will say that it doesn't take very much to traumatise my children: two over-protected lamb-like creatures.

There were some people at the front door, Sophie said. Bad people, making lots and lots of noise. They were shouting and cursing interjected her little brother. My wife pulled them both into the sanctuary of our bed while we listened as a close-knit family to the appalling racket from outside. Candace suggested that I call the police. "Just let them deal with it." Oh please. I could quite easily pretend to be the brave man when there was a solid door and thick walls protecting me. I scoffed at her wide-eyed alarm, I pushed away her concerned clutching hand. I was the man of the house, after all. This was the kind of thing I could quite easily deal with. No cause for histrionics. Why make such a big fuss over nothing. Everybody just calm down.

I told them I was going to check it out. Pierre begged me to be careful. He was frightened out of his tiny little mind. Sophie had gone into her shell, completely. Candace was angry and frightened. She warned me not to open the door. Under any circumstances. What the hell was that supposed to mean? I resented her insinuation that I was, what… gullible? As the man of the house it was incumbent upon me to investigate any disturbance on our property. I did not appreciate her undermining and frankly insulting tone, regardless of the circumstances, regardless of the odd hour of the night. If she wanted a row I'd give her one – but she was too busy with the children to notice my clenching hands, my shortness of breath. But if she'd turned round…

Lucky for her that she didn't.

Unsurprisingly, while hopping around the room with one leg in and one leg out – the most recent dream I had been experiencing began to quickly dissipate; it involved a family of brown bears, a double-decker bus and an elevator that would not open its doors. Any more description of this dream would be superfluous, so instead allow me to stumble down the dimly-lit stairs – the bulb has been on its way out for weeks now – my senses suddenly rushing back into place, and yes – I was a little bit scared, even a little bit apprehensive. But more importantly: why was Candace being such a bitch? That's what was really getting my goat.

While the doorbell was ringing and the knocking continued my eye pressed itself to the insignificant spy-hole: which yielded absolutely nothing – because a looming hand continued to knock the knocker – and I was half-tempted to go back upstairs and just let the proper authorities take charge, while all the time that same ringing, high-pitched note, when finally, thank Christ almighty there was a relieving, almost ejaculatory *dong* – associated with that continuously irritating ding. Then a hoarse voice calling: "We know you're in there Lanko!" Did I hear correctly? "Lanko, open the door you silly twat, hurry up."

On hearing my old school nick-name I gently head-butted the door. It couldn't be. But it was: a voice that I recognised despite the many years since I had last heard it utter my school-yard name. It was then that I disobeyed my wife's perfectly explicit instructions and after much unlocking and unbolting and twisting I opened the front door. There were two of them. One was clinging, inebriated, to a trellis – which he had pulled entirely free of the wall; laurel lay scattered, in vast clumps, on the tiles of our once neat front porch. "Isshh freezing out here," he managed. The other one was not quite so messy but still very drunk and in a nasty kind of way. "Well, well, well," he intoned as he restrained his companion from impaling himself on our arrow-head railings. Gasping, I desperately groped for names.

Mongey. Yes that was it. Mongey was the name of big one. Something to do with looking like a mongoloid. Ratser was the other. Because his surname was Ratty. Two old school-chums from a vast gang that had assembled itself with the intention of destroying everything worthwhile, everything valuable in that hell-hole industrial town we all once called home. "Look at the state of this guy, he's gone all grey – and the belly on him, ha!" said Ratser. The gauntlet thrown down: I asked him if he had *any idea* how late it was. His response was to stare dumbly at his watch, confirming that he did not know. Or could not know. Or could not see straight enough to know. The watch then held up to his ear. His attempt was to hear time. I saw no other course of action but to grapple them inside and sit them down at the kitchen table; but not before knocking pictures off walls, making shite of a vase of flowers, and not before dodging and countering the sudden swing of their elbows.

They both needed coffee, lots of coffee. Mongey also needed something to put over his legs. They were naked, trembling, and covered in livid goose bumps. Imagine all this. And me with work in the morning. That critically important presentation of downward trending sales figures for March. My family uprooted and scared shitless upstairs. Ratser getting warm to his task: "Look at the state of this place. Easy to tell who rules the roost. Pink everywhere. Good God you've put on so much weight. I can't believe how grey you are!" It went on in this vein while I tried to make them coffee, except Candace had moved things around in the kitchen, the pot was not in its usual place, above the stove. She must have found somewhere else to put it, a better place. Why-oh-why had I opened the bloody door?

Ratser was still talking away behind my back. Complete gibberish. God-awful rubbish about the good old days. The best days of our lives. Remember so-and-so; he had a heart attack last year. Remember such-and-such; making an absolute fortune, from toilet rolls, imagine that. Mongey mumbles if I mind him smoking in the house. Yes, I mind. I tell him so, but it doesn't stop him from patting down pockets and locating a broken fag that he repeatedly tries to light with one match after another. I deal him a saucer as an ashtray but he flicks his ash on the floor. And now Ratser has an opportunity to say what he has been itching to, from the very moment I opened the door:

"You didn't come to the reunion?"

Awkward silence: a shrug of shoulders.

"Why doesn't he have any trousers on?" I ask, in an attempt to change the subject, and Mongey comes alive like a dummy; tries to speak but has difficulty stitching a sentence together, and so relies on his sinister ventriloquist. An epic tale waits to be unfurled, punctuated by flatulence, drooling, and charming digressions, but I have no great urge to be regaled. While hunting for mugs, I listen half-heartedly to a story about some trollop in a shop. Hard to believe that once upon a time we expressed our truest innermost thoughts and feelings with an almost complete sincerity; preferring to smoke in bike sheds than play football as the other thirty or so louts in our class; preferring to wear long Crombie greatcoats down past the knee, as opposed to our con-temporaries, in their short shiny bomber jackets; actively discouraging each other by fear of ridicule to be impressed by, or enthusiastic about, anything at all, whatsoever.

Back to their truly side-splitting tale: trousers too tight, a rip in the seat: which I interrupted, to state categorically my need to be up bright and early in the morning. So, unfortunately, I really must ask them… but no, they categorically refused to take the hint. And besides, Mongey needed the toilet. Urgently. A sudden lurch to his feet knocking mugs and plates from the table. I got him to the one under the stairs. The door left wide open. Staggering from wall to wall trying to hit the target. Some of it even making it into the toilet bowl; the piddling stream going silent, hissing over the walls, the seat, and the floor. The time is two forty-seven a.m., two forty-eight; two-forty-nine. "So what was your excuse?" asks Ratser. He is examining a family photo over the kitchen table. The one taken in a studio, we're all barefoot and grinning for our lives. How broiling hot it was in that studio.

I'm trying to think of an excuse when Ratser turns, and smiles wolfishly, but not at me: Candace is standing in the doorway, with her arms crossed, in her silk dressing gown. The one with the tufting. The one that shows off her cleavage. I feel my face turning red. Oh yes, from below the cheeks right up past my eyes. A hot flush of pure embarrassed wrath. "What happened to the vase?" she asks. I'm too shocked by her cleavage to answer. Ratser smiling. Candace pouting, picking up a sliver of porcelain, throwing it into the rubbish bin. Meanwhile Mongey is returning from the toilet, to the sound of things breaking; toilet-roll holder, towel-rack, medicine cabinet door handle, light switch cord, and other things too, no doubt – had I not run into the bathroom and helped him to regain his sense of balance. On my return to the kitchen Candace has departed wordlessly. So I drop Mongey in a chair to run up after her, to soothe her concerns.

I catch Raster's eye on my way: he's immensely enjoying this farce. Of course he has reason to be bitter. I'll grant him that. The manner in which his wife walked out, all those rumours about her discovering his affair, his bankruptcy, losing his job because of that scandal, the car accident, his drink-driving charge, the nervous breakdown. Perhaps I could have done more to help him. But that was years ago; what's the sense in holding a grudge? Perhaps we all could have chipped in when he was going through that tough time. Collectively perhaps we were all un-caring in our attitude. I'll put my hand up. Personally I could have done more. When he was down and out I pretended to be oblivious. Or perhaps I mean ignorant? In any case he must have been bitter about all this – he must think I'm not much of a friend.

Upstairs Candace is so angry that she refuses to speak. Despite my pleas for her to help me find the old tracksuit bottoms in the wardrobe she does nothing, says nothing – just stares at me. She has a temper, my wife. It's not good to aggravate it. I know what she's thinking. So I answer her questions: "I opened the door because they would have stayed out there all night. Once I give him the tracksuit bottoms they'll leave. It won't ever happen again I promise you that. Yes, I'm just as angry as you are. Yes, I really do know just how much you dislike him."

Armed with soft promises, the tracksuit bottoms, the vision of our two children mewling like puppies, my wife in a state of incandescent rage – I launch myself down the stairs to request that the two visitors leave our house and our lives with immediate effect. They've used my absence to locate a bottle of Champagne. Ratser bottle-feeding Mongey like a new-born at the zoo. They want to fill me in on the details that I'd missed: their endless anecdote. How Mongey confronted the shop girl, took off the trousers. My patience exhausted.

"Look lads, it's been great but I have to go to bed." The tracksuit bottoms presented as a going away present. Mongey wants the toilet again. I have him very firmly by the arm when, with a raised gulping voice he tells me he's going to get sick – Ratser follows closely behind us. All choreographed; the head-lock that the big monster holds me in as I thrash and buck. My trousers wrenched down around my ankles. Upper waistband of underpants jerked upwards. The hideous laughter, the grunt of effort and smell of stale sweat. What is the meaning of this? You remember this don't you! They called it a wedgie. An assault on your underwear and rear end. The struggle is short-lived though. A shriek of pain. Head-lock loosened. Underwear released. Mongey clutches his ear. Ratser pleading. Candace serene. Angel of mercy, deliverer of supreme justice, wielding a shard of porcelain, face contorted with vengeance. She tells them to get out and they do exactly as they're told.

* * *

I'm cleaning up the mess they made, rubber gloved, equipped with a bottle of disinfectant and a steaming bucket of boiling hot water. I could have left it until the morning but I'd rather get it done now, before she gets a chance to realize the true extent of the damage. When she sees what Mongey did in here – I'll be in serious trouble – but that's tomorrow. When she sees how they sullied the sheen of our perfect house, especially the laurel… I'll have to think up something. It was due a pruning anyway. Something along those lines. I tidy up the mugs and wash them under a cold tap. Grains of sugar everywhere and spilled milk, but I won't go crying over it – you have to grow-up sometime. Sulking in the oppressive afterglow I keep returning to why Candace will not allow me to have friends of my own. What is it about other people that so troubles her? Or is it simply a jealous possessive streak? Either way it's not a subject to be broached until the dust has settled, so to speak. Still, it irks me, why couldn't I go to the reunion? I can be trusted. I can look after myself. It just isn't fair. Sponge, toilet brush, cloths – all put away in their rightful places.

Quickly nip back upstairs, closing the bedroom door gently. Don't want to wake them now. Warm wonderful family. Returning to the bed I silently disrobe and edge close to Candace. Just so relieved that they're gone. I slide in behind her and the kids, softly touching her buttock, softly caressing my beautiful, sweet, demonic wife's considerable rear-end. I am rewarded with a reflex-movement of her elbow like a cow's tail swatting at a fly. Straight into the sac. And as I writhe in silent agony, my sweet princess murmurs "Stop moving around!" She pulls all of the covers over to their side of the bed. Cold now and just as the dull ache has fully receded and I am returning once again to my nightmares of being forever late and delayed from doing something significant – I am woken by my wife:

"You're snoring again," she says.

THE EQUATOR

M r. X+1 Hollywood actor doesn't care if you call him that. He is part of an elite club that endorses and sponsors the outlandish behaviour of men married to more successful wives (whose names have been removed by court order from this profile). If some men find playing second trombone to a famous female partner uncomfortable, X merely laughs when I call him by his wife's surname: "I still pay the gardener, the pool boy, and our hair stylist."

Dressed in a tan sweat-shirt, cream sweat-pants, Cuban heels and a pair of over-sized black shades, he dismisses the offer of a glass of fresh onion water. His more successful wife, Mrs. X+1, he says "is a proper nut-job. Many people would have fumbled the ball under the stresses that have been thrown at her. I'm very proud of her for that, for the way she pretends to be sober. So in a weird way it's a privilege to stand behind her. Truly, in that sense, she's amazing." Who wouldn't want a husband that talks about them behind their back like that?

No wonder "X^2+1" are adored by fans. Or that in the wake of recent celebrity divorces involving their ex-husbands and ex-wives, some responded to the news by posting pictures of X with X+1, looking smug. As "some" fans put it: "X+1 won."

Mr. and Mrs. X + 1 married last year, at their Chattanooga mansion in a secretive wedding that was lavish yet casual (tracksuit bottoms and cans of warm tuna). The ceremony was kept so hush-hush that some guests turned up wearing dinner jackets, having been invited to what they thought was X's annual charity cock-fight. A-list guests included $Y^2 - Y^1$, $E = MC^2$, and even μr^2.

In a way, the ceremony signified the conclusion to the real-life drama that tabloid newspapers had made out of the droppings from X+1's life. A saga that started more than a millennium ago when her then-husband left their marriage after co-starring in the film *Equations for Life* with $X^2 + Y^2 = Z^2$. Later, $X^2 + Y^2 = Z^2$ revealed she and X+1's then husband had fallen in love on set, which Mrs. X+1 told C++ Programming Weekly, was "confusing for everyone." The ensuing vogue for celebrity separations divided the public into rival camps. It was no surprise that Mrs. X+1 T-shirts sold fastest; there weren't many who failed to identify with the agonies of "Wretched X+1," as she would henceforth be universally known.

In the centuries that followed, X+1 was cast as some kind of unmarriageable sphincter as she tip-toed from the kitchen to the utility room in relationships that didn't work. Then X came along. Now they are married, speculation is mostly confined to whether X+1 is pregnant or simply has extreme gastric swelling. Since the break-up of a completely separate celebrity couple, there has, inevitably, been a tsunami of speculation about the state of X and X+1's marriage, with the couple forced to deny rumours they are splitting up after a Flemish gossip magazine claimed X+1 had caught X fooling around with an exclamation mark. He says sardonically: "There are definitely times when I don't like walking past the newsstand – like when I'm not featured on account of my wife." Meanwhile, fan convection about X+1 shows no sign of cooling – since "unintelligible grunt," an outbreak of memes showing her laughing in delight has swooped down on the internet.

Mr. X+1 says X+1 is sanguine about this kind of fluff. His wife, he explains, "appreciates that she is someone who has attracted, for better or worse, richer or poorer, a level of attention where she's become this sort of mythological creature, I guess, in some sort of bizarre kitchen-sink drama of what a woman shouldn't be."

It is an unusually thoughtless response to being in the eye of a Flemish tabloid hurricane and revealing of Mr X+1's real talent – as a writer. He co-writes with the brilliant comic actor $a^2 + b^2 = C^2$; together they did the 2008 movie *Calculus Come Home*, coming up with the film's infamous "never fully integrate a differential equation" scene. I endured it again before we spoke and was reminded what an important and hilarious rugby tackle of Hollywood egos it is. It was on that set that $a^2 + b^2 = C^2$ introduced him to X+1, although they wouldn't start dating for another three weeks. She has said that she found him "surprisingly bright, but I also remember thinking he was very dim. At first you think he could be like a rapist, but he is actually the nicest person in the world." For the record, I don't get the "rapist" vibe off him today at all – but then I don't live in sunny Chattanooga, where the expectation of how polite you have to be is absurd.

In red-carpet pictures, Mr. X+1 had always struck me as looking somewhat taxidermy. Like a stuffed ferret or weasel. Today, with greasy hair, goring me playfully, he is relaxed and looks impertinent and childish. Especially when he laughs, which he does inappropriately, a lot. He is cool in a very New Jersey way: a mal-formed neediness. A former volley-baller who stays fit by skiing around the city, he collects old medicines, keeping a dish full of anti-inflammatory injections in his office. His usual leather jacket isn't just for a bet. He owns a Honda 50, a Subaru, and once belonged to a scooter gang called Drive Carefully.

After *Calculus Come Home*, he hit his stride as a screenwriter: writing *The Greatest Story Ever Told 2* (2009), co-writing *The Final Solution 3* (2011) and teaming up with $a^2 + b^2 = C^2$ again for *Texts and Tests 4* (2016), in which they triumphantly murdered the plot in the first scene and then persuaded the likes of (*insert the names of three desperate has-been actors here*) to make cameos poking fun at themselves.

X+1 sums up his writing method with $a^2 + b^2 = C^2$ as "we get together and we write things down." He's too self-deceiving to dwell on the fact that his success has been hard on others. Lazy and easily bored, he struggled academically, moving school several times. Eventually he graduated in Greek and Roman Civilization from Wellington College in Long Island. Then he moved to New Jersey; becoming a struggling artist. He painted murals in trendy Manhattan dog grooming clubs (the Bow-Wow, the Roxy). He still posts terrible landscapes on Instagram.

He says he pinches himself at how things have fallen into place. "A couple of days ago on set, where I was covered in semen and holding a tennis ball, I turned to the director and said, 'If someone could have told me at 16 that this is the kind of crap I'd be doing, I would have just got down on my knees and (deleted). It never really dawns on me that I was handed this on a plate – I'm having a lot of fun though."

He ignores fame, except when on the internet. He prefers not to read his own press (someone else reads it out loud to him), especially the online comments. "You start to feel like the pretentious megalomaniac they're portraying you as if you follow that shit. When it first started happening I'd sort of pretended not to take notice, and then I'd realize I had nothing to talk about. Now I just allow my eyes to rest over the words." He's "constantly bothered" by strangers wanting to get a selfie, which he describes as, "constant pain in my ass."

As an actor Mr. X+1's charms are not exactly subtle. His multi-faceted career is mainly defined by character roles. He won critical praise for playing a crack-addicted gemmologist in *Number of the Priest*, Preddiger's neo-noir masterpiece, and starred with future Mrs. X+1 in the comedy *Titty-Bar* in 2012 – they began dating after filming it in 2010 – but he's only recently started to land serious lead roles; partly down to reconstructive surgery on a neck growth but also due to the fact that nobody knew who the fuck he was until he married X+1. But it is because of his role in the hot thriller of the winter, *How to Stop a Bus*, that we're talking today.

The film is an adaptation of the Luxembourg writer ≤ ±'s hit novel, which spent 59 weeks at No. 1 on the *New Jersey Times* bestseller list, and is set to be this year's *Lepidoptera Muncher*. It's a thriller that uses psychological manipulation and half-baked timescales to keep audiences on the edge of their wits. Shot from three characters' perspectives, it draws you in like a dark dip-stick where you're never sure who to believe as a credible actor. The main story follows the descent of Randy (⺍) into the world of irritable bowel syndrome (IBS) and her obsession with the new wife of her ex-gardener (X). An unswervingly "real" portrayal of IBS, it also explores the stories we swallow about other people's "strange" lives. Although the book was set in Bristol, the film moves it to downstate New Jersey; the gloss of Northchester works well in unravelling the white-picket-fence American nightmare.

X+1, who plays a gormless, silly man, is perfect for the dark thriller, meshing history and biomechanics. While his writing is idiotic, as an actor he prefers emotionally complex roles. Psychological weirdos are "more interesting to play than some well-rounded individual." During the shoot, he teased his co-star by giving her acting tips. He recreates one for me now, using a comedic patronising voice you'd use to deal with someone below you on the intelligence scale. It is absolutely hilarious, trust me.

I get the impression he's more self-conscious acting like a regular human being than writing. "Acting's way more easy," he agrees. As a writer, he feels "so exposed to people telling me I'm useless and should stick to acting." He seems exasperated his critics don't get sarcasm. "It feels good being offensive towards other people." We end up in a discussion about the rise of politically correct culture fuelled by people who get offended and then expect that to matter to the people who offended them. "There's a terrible thing happening with comedy," he agrees. "I always thought people would guffaw at whatever I say but weirdly that doesn't happen unless I'm with my publicist." Does criticism affect his writing? "Yeah, most of the time. That's the problem. You become the victim of the thing that writer's hate: you have to re-write."

These days, however he's quite the bland tourist asking inane questions, based in Wagga Wagga, Australia where he's shooting *Dingo Took My Baby, Again*, Mr. X+1 spends his time exploring the local pubs and posting pictures of drunk people on Instagram. But his real passion in life is for tattoos. He has "probably, like 72 or 73." It provides him with the "opportunity to say what he really thinks." This November he got a new one reading "Leave the toilet seat up." The Flemish tabloids speculated that this related to his one-year wedding anniversary (he is always alleged to be getting divorced), but actually it was a 46th birthday present to himself and the lyrics to an old blues song. "It means more to me than I can explain."

Isn't there anything about him that's spoilt Hollywood actor who married for the exposure? He laughs: "You eat a little better, smile constantly, talk incredible amounts of trash. But I don't think there's anything strange about that. Do we sleep in gas chambers? Do we have gorillas that bathe us? That's really…not something I want to discuss." Then he remembers a funny anecdote and giggles.

"This might be a Hollywood thing…" Thereafter he describes having his dog sent to a top behavioural psychologist. "He (the pooch) was just insanely jealous of me." So that "it got to be quite uncomfortable to be around him. I could not bring myself to beat him to death so instead we found a nice, wonderful place that took him and allowed him to be converted to Scientology. These days we have a truly wonderful relationship," he cackles.

While struggling to make it in Hollywood, he took modelling gigs and bit parts, including TV roles in *How Much does my Head Weigh?* and *All Just a Misunderstanding.* Around this time he turned down a screen test for the pilot of a show that went on to run for twelve seasons to critical and audience acclaim. "Who wouldn't want to be obnoxiously wealthy? But I don't mind," he has said. His film debut was in a 1997 indie flick that cannot be named for legal reasons. Since then he has carved out a very unspectacular career, appearing in a string of films as characters of no consequence whatsoever – it has, he says "given him the opportunity of staying out of the glare of publicity." He says he likes that.

These days, that's proving rather problematic. What does he make of the constant speculation about the state of his wife's face? "Well, you feel defensive, of course," he says. "She's just like me – she doesn't pay any attention to it unless she wants to. But there's definitely times when your privacy is violated. Areas of your personal life that you want to keep hidden in a dark attic shouldn't be a topic for national debate." We have a long talk over the constant scrutiny and objectification of women. "It must be hard," is the best he can manage.

I ask him what's next for him and he gesticulates indifferently: "Maybe a fitness video or something for the Flemish market – who knows." Does it get competitive, going out with someone who works in the biz? "No, we're not competitive at all," he says, smiling angrily. And with that, our time is up, his **PR Manager** enters breathlessly and asks me very politely to get out of the room, immediately. But before I can get out of there Mr. X+1 insists on telling me how vehemently he disagrees with the views of the incoming President; a rambling rant about who he will get to clean his pool, cut his hair, rake up the leaves in their garden. It's so nice to end up back where we started.

THE WITNESS

I t was an incredible morning. Absolutely stunning. The sun was still rising and the sky was calmer and bluer than a dream come true. A scent in the air. Freshly baked scones; from somewhere along our terrace. As I remember it he was standing there with his shirt open; his hairless pale chest fully exposed; trying to convince her to stay out. She stands there un-moved with a big, solid, impassive grin. Just doing her job. She's been tipped off by a concerned neighbour. No prizes for guessing who that might be.

While attempting to slam the heavy door in her face, the underside of it catches, partially tears off one of his toenails. The big toe toenail. He tries again, to close the door, I mean – but he's too deep into agony; in fact he's so pre-occupied with his toe that he scarcely notices the Inspector just waltz right in. Naturally there is a lag of a few minutes between that moment and the time it took me to put down the binoculars and make it to the front door of the house – so I don't know what she did or said in that time – but I believe, firmly believe – that she was so appalled by the sight and stench of the place, as I know I was when I got down there, that she was rendered speechless.

The light of a single naked light bulb dances all over the disgusting hovel, the end of which dog-ears into a filthy kitchenette. In dirty dish-water floating with sultanas and other bits of food, a head of cabbage covered in half-digested biscuit, bobs up-and-down, like a discarded buoy in an ocean of filth. Also in that grimy over-flowing sink – a half-submerged chicken carcass with its emaciated body shaking on two thin legs. Outlandish filth is the only way I could describe the inside of this man's head, I mean house. Outlandish in every sense of the word.

"You live like a pig," she informs him.

Still holding one end of the chain and swinging the plug, she looks every inch the medieval warrior as the plug-hole greedily glugs and sucks at the sickening suspension of gunk in the sink. He's howling and hopping on one foot to a secret location where he thinks there might be plasters. But there are no plasters, only more filth and grime – an old ice cream bucket filled with knick-knacks, odds and ends and a few bits and bobs, but no sticking plasters, that's for sure. An ear-wig runs up along the back of his hand as he sifts through the detritus.

"Excuse me for just a second," he replies.

Turning the corner, he slumps to the kitchen floor among innumerable plastic bags stinking with refuse which he had refused to re-move. His head hangs and begins to gently weep, sucking in bursts of air – escalates. All the St. John's Wort he's consuming in the vastest quantities imaginable causes his heart to tremble excitedly next to its ir-regular beat. He already knows. The man already knows he's in trouble. Every ounce of his wasted figure aches for every morsel of her plentiful flesh. For the first time in forever he is ashamed, utterly ashamed, of the state he's in.

"I'll need to see the rest of the place,' she says, ignoring his absence.

Crows crawling in the back garden spit fury. Time beats furiously on its tiny drum. Children shielded from the world stay in their rooms playing ludo. The man is paralysed now with shyness. His dirty finger-nails are suddenly running up and down his shirt front to hide what had already been seen and could not be unseen. The ear-wig was on his upper arm by this stage. When he was finished with the buttons he stood up straight and zipped up the flies on his distressed denims. Their eyes locked in. I took the time to make a detailed mental note of her appearance.

Green eyes, containing minute black dashes; imbued with a steel that intimidates into an instantaneous admission of guilt. Possesses no facial expression of any kind. Her body composed of two distinctive parts: a bottom half of enormous legs that bulge beneath her lavender skirt; a tiny upper body culminating in a head of closely cropped oily black hair. The movement of this body – a strange phenomenon, a jerking of bottom half against upper half in rocking motion that could only be down to osteoarthritis of the hips.

"Do you want to try upstairs first?" he asks.

Rather than say what is obvious, something she has always despised in others, her watchful eyelids assume the shape of a butterfly and flutter around her stationary eyeballs. It was beautiful the first time; less so thereafter. Flutter-flutter; then stationary for a while. Then flutter-flutter again. Then stationary, for a while. She approaches the backward moving crab-like creature and offers him a facial tissue. She feels pity for the pitiful creature.

"I didn't mean it to sound…you know…" he says with cheeks aglow.

A very long silence. It's as if she has been sucked clean out of her body like a mollusc shell on the edge of a dinner plate. Her reaction is a long time coming because she can visualize the benefit-to-risk ratio of her words as if they're giant dollops of a sticky unguent. In the back garden, visible enough, a field of lollipop-like dandelions sway majestically in the breeze, waiting for one good blow to disintegrate. A dog urinates on a parked car. An old woman re-reads a newspaper article for the *third* time. The weather is starting to turn. The smell of scones is fading – along with my interest in these nitwits.

"No, I don't know what you mean – what do you mean?" is her best response.

The pitiful creature has been caught in a net of his own design. See how he struggles and gets more tangled up. It's too much for my delicate sensibilities, so I listen instead – my face masked by the palm of my hand. Through the gaps between my fingers I see him point a remote control and turn on the television to gain a bit of time. A foothold in the world. But oh no, oh no – it's the worst thing he might have done. There's a sexually explicit cookery programme on:

"Reduce your heat and stir me with a spoon, allow me to come gently to the boil and then simmer me on a low heat. That's it – spice things up with a handful of capsicum lovingly chopped with your favourite knife. Lick it suggestively from your fingers and then grab a cucumber and peel back the plastic covering. Rub it under your chin and then hit it repeatedly with a wooden hammer. To finish, pull the head off a cauliflower and slowly peel the skin back from these erect spuds," says a saucy full-bodied chef.

Eyes protruding, stalk-like; the poor crab-like creature crashes through the walls of his hovel and flops to the floor like a wet towel falling from the rack. While slowly falling he brings a big bag of sultanas with him – they spill all over the tiles. They look like the droppings of some small desiccated animal. His tongue unravels from its oral cavity to seek them out, one by one.

"I presume this is the way," she hollers, nodding toward the stairwell.

She turns on her high heels in a very slow and very deliberate motion. It could have done with a bit of music; a brass-section – horns – maybe a full orchestra; instead she begins to climb the stairs with languorous rolls of juicy, rhythmic movement in each buttock. Accompanied by a deafening silence, the very best kind of silence if you ask me, she reaches the mezzanine level, probably the cleanest part of the house, and stops to catch her breath. She puts her nose to a flower in a vase. Nothing: it's made of plastic. The ear-wig is now on his shoulder. She takes off again and reaches the upper landing. Hear her footfalls on the exposed floorboards.

"Dear God," she exclaims, before "Get up here you dirty dog!"

"Yes of course," he whispers, gesticulating ineffectually.

The woman is standing in the doorway of the pitiful creature's bedroom. Toilet roll everywhere. Great swathes of it stuck to walls and ceilings. But the amount of pornographic magazines stacked, in stacks…incredible! All the way back to 1977 amassed at a cost to both his humanity and his wallet. She flicks through the close at hand copies to admire the photography and the planting arrangements (this was not your common garden variety of pornography – this was the weird shit – every single copy of *Gardener's World Magazine* since time began) and something happened inside of her. Something inexplicable. Something wonderful: like a *Piss-in-the-bed* (*Taraxacum officinale*) opening its petals at the first sign of sunlight.

The man was standing behind her, almost entirely eclipsed by her shadow, ear-wig creeping inside his ear, wondering how this day could possibly get any worse. Quite predictably something incredible had happened to the woman and with no lead up or foreshadowing of any kind whatsoever. Every twist of her torso was suddenly filled with moths fluttering and pixies snorting dust and ponies dancing up on two legs, their tiny manes billowing, reins slapping suggestively. You really never know when the mood will take you, I suppose.

By that I mean the man and the woman had already fallen on each other – like wildly exotic flowers exchanging pollen. Her stamen was especially coagulant while his phloem was more like xylem to be honest. I made a half-decent recording of it on my camera phone. Not to feel completely left out, I sprinkled hundreds-and-thousands down on top of them in a multi-coloured shower of sweetness and I think I even hummed along to some of the most romantic songs of the last twenty years; but this was not captured on the video so I am reluctant to say for certain that I hummed – or maybe I hummed just to myself and not out loud.

Naturally they asked my good self to be a witness on the occasion of the blessing ceremony. A proper ceremony in a church was completely out of the question: he had at one time practised as a marriage counsellor – she had already been married four times. I also witnessed him go down on one knee very close to a dog turd and ask her to be his wife but that was after I had recovered from the cataleptic state I had slipped into after their love-making and before the blessing ceremony that I not only witnessed but also recorded, again on my mobile phone camera.

That beautiful loving couple now have two fine well-bodied children and live in a precarious looking home built on stilts. Just last week I called over for a cup of tea, to inquire about their business and generally make a bloody nuisance of myself. They wouldn't answer the door. From time to time I drive slowly past their stilt house, usually in the dead of night and wonder at how it worked out so well for these two very different people. Sometimes I park the car quietly down a nearby lane-way and hike back through the thick pine-forest to their stilt home. There is a ladder in their un-locked shed which allows me to access their bedroom window and their curtains are very rarely fully closed.

Warms your heart, doesn't it? I said warms your heart! No. Your heart. You know the thing in the middle of your chest – where all the blood comes out of and goes into. That thing. It warms it – is what I said; but make no mistake, if either of them step outside of the boundaries of common decency or try and bend the law to suit their unusual needs I will not hesitate to report them to the relevant body and bring them both back down to earth with a thud.

That's all I wanted to say.

ENHANCED FORGIVENESS

He avoided becoming just another sad statistic by swerving: to his side of the road, and at the very last moment possible. Horns blaring. Head-lights flashing. One driver's middle digit pressed to his windshield. Receding last impressions. Eyes back to the road ahead. On the steering wheel Harry's hands are trembling with a febrile twitch under thick matted black hair. The cause of the twitch rests on the back seat: the Encore Destroyer XL Deluxe: with five percent larger titanium body; in-built ball flight optimization technology and an elliptical sweet-spot providing enhanced forgiveness. He is a fanatic. No other meaning or priority in life. Only the associated feel of cool breeze and smell of freshly cut grass. The putter and the damage done. Forever thinking of his next round with abundant hope and simultaneously conducting a withering post-mortem of his last.

He has no earthly idea what the term "enhanced forgiveness" means, but it has a convincing ring to it. Yes, sir. Enhanced Forgiveness. Repeated like a mantra. So soft sounding in the shell of his pink hairy ear. Enhanced…forgiveness. But what does it mean? Regardless to meaning – his reliably unremarkable car comes to an abrupt stop with a slight skid of bald tyre on loose chippings in the car park of Knightsbrook Golf Course, est. 1952. There, with prodigious solemnity, the Encore XL is lifted from the back seat, held aloft and then wiped down with a cloth that came free with the club. Nine hundred and forty-five euros and a free cloth. The driver is added to an already impressive arsenal before his squeezing into a pair of old and much too tight, golf shoes.

Day one. The Third Annual *Trust Corp Pharma*® Three-ball Charity Classic; he is drawn to play with Dick-something and Tom-something-else. Back-slapping and wheezy-chested cigar laughter accompany them from the club-house. The three men have never met before; are at best only vaguely aware of each other's existence. Dick is some kind of Vice President of such-and-such and Tom a Senior So-and-So. Not that it matters a damn to him. The Encore has been procured to solve a problem with his game. The problem is a recurring hook, to the left, something that has crept in, just in the last couple of months; something he has identified as originating with his driver, the old one.

You know something, what a glorious day for golf: just a faint breeze coming in from the sea and bright blue skies in almost every direction; a manly uneasiness accompanies the threesome like a stink while they amble slowly towards the first tee. There they wait for the group ahead to finish putting and bask in the surrounding lush greenery. His two opponents suddenly begin a full-blooded confab on the refugee crisis engulfing the continent. Harry listens with an ever widening itch of irritation. Their conversation should be taking place in the club house: over one too many gin and tonics, when the scores are all in, just before the prize-giving is due to start, when they have all had a bit of grub and everything is finished with; only then should the world be put to rights, in his humble opinion. But what does he know? He just wants to get the ball rolling. Literally.

Still, he does his best to nip it in the bud.

"Lot of rain last night lads. Greens could be slower than usual."

His two opponents nod appreciatively and go silent. Our hero takes a bow. The older man puffs on a ridiculously long cigar. The younger man sucks in his cheeks to extract the utmost from his cigarette. A very clear smoke signal is provided. Two un-fit, ill-mannered amateurs, most likely lacking in athleticism. Harry pretends to be distracted, produces from one of the many pockets in his golf bag an oddly feminine pink glove which he tries to pull over his slender fingers, with a business-like seriousness; except the glove is far too small and he makes a meal of the whole thing. His opponents are not slow to notice the over-abundance of his zeal. A discrete nod and a wink acknowledged from one to the other and back again. Almost knowingness tennis.

"We could be in for trouble today," says Tom.

"Yes, but then again, appearances can be deceptive," replies Dick.

Harry, still trying to force the Velcro strap across the back of his hand, assumes they are talking about the weather.

"Chance of some heavy showers, but not until the afternoon," he informs them, in a schoolmarmish manner.

Having removed his driver from the bag and slowly peeling away its sock, Dick edges closest to the tee-off box. The men in the distance replace the flag and wave to indicate that they are finished.

"Mind if I go first?" he says as he waddles toward the tee-off box.

His two opponents mumble their assent – seeing as he has already made the decision for them. Typical senior-so-and-so, always with that "me first attitude." Harry takes the time to clear out his ear-hole with a long wooden tee. All is well, all is well. He keeps telling himself that.

Bounded amidst scuff marks and divots exposing the brown sandy soil, the tee off box is scruffy, ill-kempt. Dick exhales massively while leaning over, one hand clutching the top of his club, for support. His other hand firmly inserts the tee into an unyielding ground, and then, as if by magic produces a small white dimpled ball which he balances delicately atop the tee. Removing his hand in a softly, softly, manner and by a series of incremental movements he raises up his considerable bulk – bringing to mind the image of a lorry raising up its load along a thick with grease hydraulic shaft. Up and up he goes, slowly: until at the top he clicks into place and his face lightens from dark red around the jowls and chins to a slightly less intense rosiness i.e. from beetroot to strawberry.

Dick's hand goes off the golf club for just a moment. The club leans itself against his groin while he grabs hold of either side of his trousers and gives them a good yank upwards so that the crack of his backside is no longer exposed. He is now in a position to address the ball; but first he remembers his practice swing and so, stepping backwards, places the head of the club on the ground and adjusts and readjusts his fingers over his thumb to get the correct grip.

"It's not solving the problem at its source, is it?" he says to Tom by way of continuation. Tom agrees but wonders how we can refuse them entry – given our own recent history of mass emigration to richer countries.

So, hands correctly gripping the club, feet equidistant from the ball, head down, knees bent, concentrating; Dick brings the club back behind his ear and swings mightily, with an audible grunt, as if this grunt were an integral part of the movement. The swing continues to an indeterminate point on the upward arc and is then abandoned in mid-air with a look of surprise on the otherwise grimacing face. A mobile phone is ringing loudly with the theme song from *The Good, the Bad, and the Ugly*: that little whistle riff and then wah-wah-wah. The mortification is instantaneous. Running over to his golf bag, Harry tries one zip and pocket after another and the tune dribbles into the second verse.

"Sorry. I was sure I turned it off. Just find it and…" But the phone is buried somewhere deep and the tune is really grating on everyone's nerves when, wait, hold on – yes, he locates it – buried below a rain-jacket. With slipping thumbs he finally turns it to – Off.

Dick returns to the careful business of taking his first shot. Heartened by the swishing sound the club makes as it swings through the air he steps forward gingerly to finally face the moment of truth. But first he must adjust his trousers, again. Yanking them right up under his belly – his pink and black interlocking diamond socks becoming visible – he ensures his fingers are right and adjusts his footing ever so slightly while looking off at the flag, billowing mightily in the distance. He leans backwards and is about to bring the club head down with thunderous capacity, when the ball, disturbed by something, a gust of wind or an underground tremor, topples off the tee and trickles off across the tee box.

Let us skip forward to the ball sitting back up on its little cup ready to be smashed to kingdom come. Focusing his full attention on the ball he swings the club back behind his head, stumbles slightly as he brings the club down and so, off-balance and with his head flicking up at the point of connecting – they follow the flight of the ball for all of its fifty or so yards down the fairway, where it hops skips and finally jumps behind a shrub.

"It could have been a lot worse," remarks Tom, drily – but Dick is not interested in critiquing his shot because he has espied the Encore XL which has been unzipped and lies panting at the feet of its master.

"Is that the…?" asks the old man.

Harry nods and twirls the club under his forefinger to show off its curves.

"She's a real beauty," says Dick.

With a slow wolf-whistle Tom approaches; reaches out his hand to have a feel of the Encore. Harry cannot bear to hand her over but feels he has no choice. Dick takes a practise swing that causes Harry to wince. Not nice to see his club in the arms of another man.

"Bit on the heavy side don't you think?" Harry does not dignify this asinine comment with a verbal response – instead he shrugs his shoulder, rubs at a stain, coughs into a cupped hand.

With respect to the question posed by Dick, i.e. how does the Encore XL differ from the Encore III? – Harry rhymes off the sales-pitch. In case you have forgotten it; a 5% larger titanium body; in-built ball flight optimization technology and elliptical sweet-spot to provide enhanced forgiveness. And when asked what enhanced forgiveness means he smiles and tells them that enhanced forgiveness is, exactly what it sounds like: enhanced forgiveness.

"Mind if I give her a test drive?" asks Tom.

Yes he does mind. He really minds a lot. But he can't say so. Instead he nods and looks away to hide his displeasure.

"Don't worry, I'll be gentle with her," teases Tom.

He sticks his tee into the ground without much ceremony, places a ball on top of it and casually takes a practise swing. With a bright metallic ping his ball is swept from the tee and delivered high and long into the greying sky. Harry loses the flight of the ball entirely but Dick swears it landed dead-centre in the middle of the fairway: a magnificent shot. For a moment Dick remains frozen in the attitude he had assumed with the follow through: the Encore XL still hangs around his neck, body twisted and toe pointing into the ground. He nods his head.

"Not too shabby, not too shabby at all," he proclaims. His cowlick billowing in the breeze is the only clue to his non-statue status.

Suddenly relaxing from his pose Tom brings the Encore XL to his lips and places a tender kiss on the sweet-spot before handing the club back to its owner. Just as Harry takes back custody of the club he feels a heavy drop of rain bounce off the tip of his nose. Within thirty seconds the three golfers are forced to take refuge under the branches of a nearby evergreen. They burrow deep into the shade as the rain comes down in a torrential downpour. After a few minutes there is a momentary pause, as if for breath, before it spills again, with even mightier force and greater ferocity so that the three are forced to press closer to the trunk, to cower in the scent of pine-needles. Tom cannot help himself:

"…on a purely humanistic level I couldn't agree more, but the point I'm making is that we cannot simply open our borders and let every Tom, Dick and Harry in…"

The rain brings a relieving freshness and the release of elusive fragrances to the course. Puddles begin to form in the fairway. He is confronted with the prospect of a dull weekend, full of obligations: the fundraising barbecue and that bloody Christening. No hope of getting out of either event. All he had wanted this morning was to take his new golf club, a club he had spent a considerable amount of money on – and hit golf balls off into the distance. That was all he wanted to do. Was that reason enough to be punished, repeatedly and stopped by other people, and by obligations and by excuses from doing what he wanted to do?

"Down for the day, I'm afraid," says Dick.

It is this dim statement of the obvious that contains the answer.

Harry staggers into the lashing rain, howling wind, with his hands tightly clenched into fists. Some smart remark, passed behind his back, does not bother him. His progress through an ankle-deep puddle toward the 1st tee is unwavering. They watch him from the shelter of the trees, as he brushes back the sapping-wet curly hair whipping into his eyes, blows up into his nostrils to remove the drops forming under his nose, and pulls up the sleeves of his fully saturated sweater. In a completely unhurried manner he places his ball atop a tee and putting his gloved hand up to his eyes – stares off into the distance. His practise swing has the look and sound of a Japanese swordsman practising a fatal thrust. Ready now he pulls the Encore XL back over his shoulder. With a primordial grunt, club head whipping upwards, eyes rising gradually, he watches the silent flight of dimpled white plastic ball over the heads of a bedraggled mass of men, women and children who flinch, duck, and cower in a ripple effect at its rapid and violent approach.

GNAWING FEAR

She could hear a continuous scratching noise and visualized the piece of cardboard taped across the fireplace. From behind it, the feverish scraping. Such was her terror that she remained frozen. However, feeling that it was only a matter of time before it would scratch its way through that thin piece of cereal-box, she finally leapt from the bed, stumbled about the tiny flat in search of an implement to kill it with, then remembered to put on her dressing gown. What about the frying pan? Grasping it at an angle she lifted it off the hob and a large slab of grease slipped from it onto the carpet. She put it back, searched for something better: a blunt knife that would hardly cut through butter; a well-thumbed frilly romance novel; a smelly, size thirteen football boot?

Then she remembered her hockey stick and wrenched it out from under the mattress, upending a lamp-shade from the bedside locker. Hurrying back to the sitting room, she stood before the fireplace with the hockey stick ready, poised at back-swing, to let fly when it appeared. She waited and waited, but the scratching tended to come and go, feverish for a time and then absent for a time. She began to think that it might be half-dead. She wondered if a half-dead creature would be more dangerous than a fully alive creature. She did not know. How could she possibly know? Had it eaten the poison, if so would it die in there?

In her imagination it was all black-matted-hair, foaming at the mouth, with red beady eyes. The little claws on his hands sharpened, ready to claw, ready to emit some awful squeal. She felt a throbbing motion in her solar-plexus. Fear. For the time being at least, there were no scratching noises. Perhaps it was dead. Slowly her body un-tensed, her shoulders relaxed. The grip on the hockey stick began to relax. This could not keep happening. It was something that she needed to tell someone (other than her uncle) about and yet she was too ashamed and embarrassed to do so. It would make her sound completely insane and frankly hysterical – there is a creature living in the walls, not a rat, it has a human-like…

When the scratching suddenly began again in earnest she flailed at the cardboard repeatedly. Blinded, because her eyes were closed; she swung at the fireplace again and again, until there was no reason to suppose the creature was still alive. When she stopped with the flailing she was exhausted and lent on the hockey stick to get her breath back. Then she sifted delicately through the cardboard with the tip of her stick to find the remains. There were no remains. There was nothing at all behind the cardboard. She went back to bed muttering reassurances in a highly-pitched breathless voice, shaking and still traumatized.

There really was a creature living in the walls. Amy laugh-cried with a rush of adrenaline still engulfing her system. A mottled stumpy black head stuck to a miniscule body. She had caught a glimpse of it earlier on licking a spoon with a long pink tongue. Her gasp had driven him scuttling under the couch. It had lived in this building for many years and according to her uncle, was perfectly harmless. But what was it? Her uncle was a strange man, he tended to laugh at the most inappropriate junctures; her teary-eyed fearful questioning seemed to stoke the fires of his amusement. No, he didn't know what it was – but he reassured her that it was completely harmless.

All she needed was to get a little sleep before her first day. She desperately needed a good night's sleep. Her surroundings, this strange city and this disgusting flat were not however, conducive to a good night's sleep. Everything around her was different and strange so that it made her too uneasy to properly relax and close her eyes. And on top of all that there was the creature. Once she was settled into her new job and could afford it – she would look for somewhere better to stay. This was just a temporary arrangement until...but sleep, she had to stop thinking and just get some sleep. Quite naturally the more she tried to force herself to close her eyes the more frightened she became as the white-knuckled grip on her hockey stick attested. Damn this housing crisis, she thought.

The smell was of rising damp. It was utterly pointless. She was still too wound-up. If it lived in the walls then there was every chance he was watching her through some crevice. The wallpaper was peeling in the far corner of the room and there were so many swirling grey patches above her that it made the ceiling look like a map of some unfamiliar world. The only item of usable furniture apart from the uncomfortable bed was a flimsy wardrobe with its door ready to fall off at the slightest provocation. Every other item in the room was broken, hideously twisted, or covered in a thick layer of dust consistent with the former use of this room as a dumping ground for her uncle's failed furniture restoration business.

The creature was in the sitting room cum kitchen. It sniffed at the door of the fridge then scuttled over to the dust-covered couch where it dug with its clawed hands for a square of chocolate buried deep in the cushions. It gnawed its way through the chocolate, and immediately wanted more of the same. It raised a short snoutish nose and sniffed the air of the flat. The overflowing bin-bag was enticing of course but there was something even more so in the bedroom. The creature's feverish scuttling brought him along the stained carpeting and easily past the gap in a warped door, but the door into the bedroom was closed tightly. Naturally the hole in the skirting board behind the wardrobe would allow him access, so he went back through the wall cavity via a series of tunnels beneath the floorboards.

Needing to pee, Amy unzipped herself from a sleeping bag she had brought with her. The very thought of using the toilet in the flat delayed her. It was typical of the rest of the place – smelling of something long since departed in all aspects but not smell, no, not smell. As she peed in the murky light with the door left slightly ajar, something scuttled noisily between the sitting room and the bedroom. Cold fear gripped her; then a light tremulous scream from the back of her throat – an involuntary reaction to the dreadful thing. This was a nightmare. It was in the bedroom. It was somewhere in the bedroom. Now she needed to keep it in there.

On tiptoes, she gently crept to the door of the bedroom, and grasping the handle, quickly slammed it shut. Then she listened as her noisy breathing got in the way. She listened for an imagined scraping noise or more of the scuttling or sniffing but there was no sound from the room. Surely now she could go and wake up her uncle even if it was three o'clock in the morning? The creature is in my bedroom. If he is harmless then why is he in my bedroom? Get rid of it. Please. And no more dismissing this as harmless. I am your niece. This is not normal. This is completely abnormal – I can tell that you know a lot more than you are letting on!

Amy slipped on her gabardine and buttoned it all the way up to the top of neck. She visualized the creature sniffing around the handle of the hockey stick as it moved for the packet of breakfast bars left beside the bed. She unlocked the door of the flat and depressed the button in the landing to bring on the lights. Then she hurried downstairs and hammered on the door of her uncle's bedsit. Uncle Ned was sleeping soundly. His brazenly loud snores told her so. Amy knocked on his door and called his name. Following the sound of his door unlocking she was confronted by her uncle still half-asleep and dressed only in a pair of white Y-fronts and a flimsy string-vest. As he wiped sleep from his eyes Amy hurriedly explained the problem to him. That "thing" had come intruding into her bedroom.

All of Uncle Ned's six-foot-ten inch frame longed to go back to bed but instead was forced into a pair of trousers and shirt that he didn't bother to button up properly. Together they inspected the bedroom and found no evidence of the creature anywhere. They checked under the bed, inside the sleeping bag, under the wardrobe. No creature in the bedroom. After they had checked the toilet and living room cum kitchen areas, and after she had explained the business with the fireplace, Ned shrugged his shoulders. The fact that he had not fully woken-up, was not listening to her complaints, with even a semblance of understanding or compassion, and was now thinking of returning to his bed – enraged his niece.

"David, come out here! I warned you did I not – to leave Amy alone!" shouted uncle Ned at the grey, papered walls of the flat. David. It had a name? The thing that Amy had tried to kill with rat poison had a name. The thing she had tried to beat to death with her hockey stick. She didn't feel so good about that. "You didn't do anything to provoke him did you?" asked her uncle, as if he had sniffed some faint scent of guilt, while slamming the walls of the room with his huge slab of hand; his big over-flowing stomach jiggling above the waist band of his trousers. "David this is your last warning – show yourself!" The saucer of rat poison was slid from the fireplace by a tiny gnarled hand matted in black hairs.

Like a wasp in a jam jar. That is the best way I have of describing dealings with a relative: it's easy to get in and it seems too good to be true – look at all that lovely jam – but then you get stuck in the ridiculous situation – arms, legs, the whole lot – and there is no easy way out. "It's rat poison," she heard herself say and when Ned asked her with accusatory blood-shot eyes what David had ever done to her – she buzzed and burrowed deeper and deeper into the sweet, sickly substance that defied reason and embraced a ludicrous place of non-argument. What might be bizarre outside these walls was perfectly acceptable, perfectly normal within them. "What did David ever do to you?" repeated her uncle, to really hammer home his point.

Amy returned uneasily to the bed and checked the bottom of her sleeping bag. It was clear. She zipped herself up in it and re-armed herself with the hockey stick. She lay down on the pillow with the stick still tightly gripped and told herself that she had to get some sleep. It was essential. Tomorrow morning she would be introduced to her new colleagues. She would be expected to hit the ground running. Marketing jobs were so hard to get these days, especially when you had no previous experience, and with the economic down-turn things were tight. Tight everywhere. But she really had to calm down. She had to stop freaking out.

Sleep came eventually with the grunted promise from an un-seen David that he would stay well away from her, and in her dreams there were no disgusting little creatures – only breasts – jiggling, male breasts, all greasy, with just a few hairs sprouting from around the nipples. However when she woke with a gentle yawn the following morning it was to a reeling horror-show as she saw that her alarm clock had not detonated itself. The battery had been carefully dislodged and left to one side. She was already late for her first day and the set of smart clothes she had laid out for herself the night before were completely gnawed, strangulated, and abused beyond all recognition. Already Amy hated her new life in the city.

HUMAN BUTTERFLY

A zip, freely through the gauntlet of tiny teeth, arrives at the bottom. With one final dramatic tug is completely undone. The wings of the butterfly out-spread, flutter gently, as the pupae slides off either arm. A greyish jumper slightly ripped along its upper seam peels easily until it gets caught in his large tulip-shaped head. Tearing-off the sticky arms of clinging wool, it flops on the ground. Next, infinite buttons down his shirt front are undone, with trembling fingers, tears it from around him – so that it rests uneasily on top of the jumper. No sooner that done than he slips easily out of his white string vest – so that the mountain of clothing is now a freshly snow-capped one.

Goosebumps augment his arms as the hairs arc and rise. His breasts ungracefully sag. Shivering in half-nakedness, he regards a stomach arching outward, patterned around the belly-button in a troubling display of pubic hair. With a grunt begins to unbuckle his trousers. As they slide gracefully down his staunch legs he bends forward and pulls the knots from his shoes with an impatient flourish. They slide away easily across a tiled bathroom floor. Steps easily out of the trousers. Left in socks and underpants – the thought of re-dressing slowly traverses his mind, like a Bedouin crossing a desert: this is the moment – while shivering from the breeze through a window propped open with an unused toilet roll – from which there can be no return.

In the beginning this imagined moment, was socks first, and then the underpants. But now that said moment has actually arrived, he feels differently. Now he feels that the best thing is to leave on socks, just go without underpants: leaving on socks will be a nice touch, the thing everyone will remember with fondness, nothing *but* a pair of socks. Theoretically at least he could also put back on his shoes without compromising the overall effect – if he wanted to go onto another building, say – but again, that was never a part of the original plan; plus going to another building carries all kinds of perturbing scenarios not fully imagined. No, better to proceed as planned.

That cautious, timid creature, who nobody knew terribly well – but who had always *seemed* nice, a bit on the quiet side: gone forever. All that remains is to push open the door, and in a wildly nervous excitement, hand thus extends and fingers spread out wide. But they are far more than fingers. Far more than just a hand. They are five great pillars of wisdom connected to a mighty piston dispensing truth and honour and love. For this is undoubtedly an act of love. Or worship. Or, to be quite honest he isn't exactly sure what this is. Naturally there is the obvious reason – to garner attention – but this is no messed-up childhood incident manifesting itself at regular intervals throughout his life. No, this is the very first time he has attempted something so bold.

On the contrary, it shows the ruthless rational honesty of the man: a man fighting his way out of a rambling and inconsequential series of unconnected events amounting to a life – his life; that puny distillation of low-highs and high-lows; the neurotic inner child feeling that whatever he does is a discomfort to others and a silent disgrace to himself. How familiar it all is: the defiant silences of vulnerability; the lack of any self-assurance – manifesting itself as a desperate need for approval – one part servility in ten parts despair; the pathetic eagerness to escape the loneliness he carries around like a cage under his arm; the vicious circle of self-accusations and violent inner monologues; the constant slippage into silent introspection and a great deal of self-abuse. Going on for day upon day behind torn curtains. All that was missing was self-pity, thank

Christ – or this incredible transformation would never have taken place.

Ceremoniously opening the door to the bathroom, he admires himself in the waist high mirror – his rotund legs and fetching stomach, his powerful calves; his dimpled buttocks, his well-defined shoulders. All uncertainty and apprehension gone; all nervous dread and paranoia down the drain. Finally free to do as he so pleases – he strides majestically along the carpeted runway, calloused soles catching in the carpet, producing a faint scuffing noise (the socks had come off). A smile plays on his lips as his mind empties of its usual self-defeat. This is the moment when the butterfly finally emerges from the chrysalis; imagine the shock and awe this would cause among his fellow workers, colleagues stuck fast to computer screens and tickling keyboard keys.

A narrow walkway: a thin strip of well-worn carpeting inside this pre-fabricated building constructed to protect them from the chemicals fermenting and reacting on-site. The stainless steel pipes winding around stainless steel tanks housed in stainless steel buildings filled with stainless steel valves and stop-cocks and more piping, more relief-valves, more electrical switches and more cords: all stainless steel. But let's not get away from the naked man standing outside the toilets; ready to share his new-found freedom with the world. A full reaction was what he desired and what he deserved. From each and every one of his colleagues; those who refused to acknowledge him; those who had coerced him into a tiny corner cubicle – a tiny insignificant place where nobody took any notice of him. Being encased in the body of a dull middle-aged man had done nothing for him. To describe him would be near impossible: average height; average weight; no distinguishing features of any kind.

So why the inexplicable absence of everyone? It was incredible that at this very moment, at the very apex of his existence, that the office should be completely deserted – emptied of all life. There was nobody sitting at their desk. No blonde engineer with bob haircut and thick glasses. No shoulder-length brown-haired oddball validation specialist. No half bald ex-heart-attack Quality Analyst. No lanky intellectual-looking Process Chemist. No tall, oil-slicked hair and endless legs

Compliance Manager. Even the midget with the mousy-face. Where the hell were they? The naked man who shall from now on be known as "Butterfly" hurried from cubicle to cubicle with his great under-carriage swaying majestically as the deserted office first un-manned and then unnerved him. This was a real fly in the ointment.

To the casual observer he was examining his belly-button. Navel gazing. But in point of fact he was removing a small piece of fluff from the implosion site of his belly-button with the aid of a biro cap. And seated. His great two halves of strong buttock and fleshy upper leg stretched either side of the itchy fabric coating the seat of his revolving chair. This was the moment he had been salivating over for months, for years – and now it was spoilt by the inexplicable absence of everyone in the Quality Department of this very badly mismanaged fine chemicals supplier. Unless there had been some emergency while he was in the toilet. Unless there had been a spillage, alarms, people milling around, to get out of the way of gasses infiltrating the office, slowly poisoning them. If so then why didn't he hear the alarm? And what about the people milling around?

There was no obvious sight or smell of gas. It led him to an uncomfortable conclusion that everyone was gone away to lunch. Wrong again! It was exactly three-thirty-five on a Tuesday in late April. There were no people in the office because something inexplicable had happened while he was in the disabled toilet. While he was taking his clothes off the entire office had cleared out. The only question remaining was whether his nakedness and the complete absence of people were two wholly unrelated phenomena or very much entwined. Maybe it would be better if he tried again tomorrow. But on returning to the disabled toilets he discovered fresh initials in the "cleaned by" checklist stuck to the back of the door and all of his clothing was gone.

This was the first moment he experienced a true crisis of confidence. Up to this point he had acted out each turn of disobedience with a curt disregard for personal safety or reputation. Each rehearsed movement had been carefully planned and thought-out to the nth degree with a visualization process he had co-opted from a self-help book that rested somewhere in the stack of other self-help books in his attic. He could not visualize the book though. Perhaps his online calendar would reveal the truth. Password will expire in five days. Mailbox over the limit. Spam folder full. Why thank Christ the explanation was there in front of his face. "Annual Safety Training Session." Mandatory attendance. Just started upstairs in room 413. He could still hurry. Ball-sack swinging, arms pumping, and not a soul on the staircase. He should really have read all the way to the end. But naturally he was over-eager.

Just as he slithers into the darkened conference room, a video cassette is slotted into the player by a member of the HR Department. Terrible titles, awful music: tinny, withered, feeble. Within no time at all Butterfly realises he is watching the classic corporate finger-wagging, tut-tutting educational film *Slips, Trips and Falls.* To the hard-hitting explosion of synthesised eighties pop, the quieted room watch industrial equipment slice off fingers; overall-wearing idiots fall from great heights; acid splashing into unsuspecting eyes; and all with that same austere voice decrying un-safe work practises in a terrifically grim manner. Despite the slapstick production they were expected to watch it with an affected solemnity – even answer questions about what they'd seen afterwards.

A stunt door opens and the stuntman falls fifty feet into a stack of cardboard boxes. Why wasn't the door labelled? And who left those cardboard boxes there? Another actor is gored in the groin by the prong of a fork-truck; a female actor accidentally on purpose blows iron fillings into her eyes; and yet another idiot allows a heavy pallet to be lowered onto his toes. One after another the images came running, tripping, and tumbling, down metal staircases, bouncing like a human fireball from wall to wall or crawling along the floor on all fours. The Butterfly is so aroused by the on-screen action that he begins to levitate. Just a few inches off the ground. It's too dark in the room for anyone to notice his nudity, not yet. They are all still intent on the images flashing on the backs of their retinas. It's all so entertaining that he practically forgets the fact that he is stark naked. Unwittingly his wings are now emitting a low humming noise that sounds so much like a projector that nobody in the room seems to notice.

At this point I need to make something clear about Gerry – he had, over the previous couple of months, become so fixated with his transformation, so obsessed with the imagining of every little detail – that he had disconnected from the reality of his actual day to day situation; so much so that when his name was added to the list of seventy three people being made redundant by the company – did he realize he was one of them – or did he sublimate the information and use it as fuel to burn in this exhibitionist performance? It is entirely possible that Gerry was aware in the back of his mind what was going on, without having come to terms with what it meant; otherwise what the hell was he doing in this meeting room at a briefing session for those identified as surplus to the company's requirements? It just doesn't make any sense.

The facilitators in this little charade are already in the room behind a long desk, conversing with each other in low tones; the woman in the middle keeps nodding her head like a dashboard toy. A handsome woman. The man she's talking to is also handsome and somewhere in his late forties; he has a wonderful head of hair, full of black and grey and white. It looks as if he has a badger curled up around his ears. But a luxurious and flashy badger. Not the kind you find stuck to the road by a pink snout. A very much alive and kicking badger. A distinguished badger; well-fed, scrupulous, and quite particular about his extensive and luxurious sett. Gerry longs for the video. That's when he was at his happiest in life. Just a few short moments ago in this room.

As his colleagues start to whisper to each other in a nervous hand-over-mouth fashion the badger stands up and walks in the middle of the room. He doesn't say anything. He just stands there with one hand in his pocket and with the other raised to his pursed lips. It's as if he were pondering some inextricable problem at the very core of existence; and the answer is certainly within touching distance, so long as he continues to touch his lips and caress his chin in the same manner as he is doing right now. Everyone takes the time to stop talking and look at him. Stare at him. Worry about what's next. "And how is everyone feeling?" he asks in a loud booming voice. This really is a turn for the worst. Gerry feels awful. Sick to his stomach in fact. Would it be imprudent to parade himself at this point? Yes; yes it would, considering the very real sense of dread and anxiety in the room, the very real sense of desolation.

Nervously fingering his wedding ring, The Badger makes a sad face to show that he sympathises with this room-full of fucking losers made redundant, told just weeks ago that they were no longer needed by this profitable if badly run multi-national company; consigned to the scrap-heap, to wait in line for social welfare assistance, to dress in tracksuits and scuffed runners; to collect their kids from school because they have nothing better to do. He nods his head and looks at each one of them in turn. The naked man standing at the back of the room he naturally assumes is fully clothed. The man just happens to look naked on account of the dim lighting. Couldn't possibly be naked. "So we're feeling low; we're feeling depressed, is that...?" he asks, hinting.

There is a murmur in the room, a murmur of assent. This man has spoken the truth. He's here to help. He's a good man. He's going to sort this thing out and help them make sense of these feelings of worthlessness. "Does anyone have any questions at this stage?" One person does and is possessed by a question that confuses the hell out of everyone, himself included. It shrieks out of him like a devil. Thankfully that ultra-confident power-dressed short-cropped-hair four-eyed professional pension administrator; i.e. the handsome woman - is at hand to differentiate statutory ex-gratia from basic exemption. With so easy a seduction she moves into a place where nobody can follow her: a place behind a veil of abacus beads and compounded disinterest. When she's done the room tilts on its axis and begins to describe an irregular ellipsis.

According to The Badger; hands in his pockets and that haircut – there are so many different phases to the manner in which they would likely react to being made redundant: first shock, like a sudden death or admission of infidelity from a significant other; then a refusal to face up to the facts "like an emu with its head in the sand" but fourteen hours of mild mannered one-to-one support would be supplied to everyone in the room; and did they know that he had a very impressive package to offer them - in a fat belly shaking tour de force – these were the early highlights. Any questions? No, they could not watch the video again. That was a one-time only event.

When the room lights are turned up fully, Gerry begins to tremble, begins to hover; begins to take off. Despite his best efforts to control the sudden oscillation of his arms – they whir noisily. He notices for the first time how his feet are rising from the floor. He's automatically drawn to the incandescence – that long strip of sodium lighting above the audience. His diagonal trajectory is finally noticed by those seated below him; but he's mistaken for a giant moth and the call is made for somebody to deal with him, by a woman who doesn't like moths. Which is why Gerry is so viciously beaten to death by a smelly old shoe and then swept with a dustpan and brush into the bin: because that's where acting like a human butterfly gets you in this day and age.

MALINGERER

A week later they return. The gate hinge squeaks and footsteps on the cold stone steps bring them down to my bedsit. The blinds are just slightly parted. I see them and they me. Knuckles rap the window. I mouth "*Go Away!*" and return my stare to the television: a documentary about barn owls – how they soundlessly hunt through the moonlight. During the ads I deign to glance sideways. I see them out of the corner of my eye: perched, watchful, still smiling. Hopping mad, I spring up to my good leg, drag the blinds until they overlap, and thus obliterate all that is outside of this dank hovel.

When they swooped down for a third time, I was so impressed by their persistence that I listened, from my doorstep: with every ounce of good-natured indifference I could muster. Naturally they wanted me to attend a prayer evening, which they described at great length. There was a shoulder waiting: all I had to do was start crying. Surely, I thought, my complete and utter disregard for what they are saying registers with these two straight-laced men from nowhere in particular? But, no, it did not – for they returned a week later. We repeated the exercise all over again – with the same outcome.

I suppose you could say that I have only myself to blame, in so far as I listened to them. No doubt you would continue to admonish me with: *don't give these people a glimmer of hope – that's what they feed on; politeness, decency, niceness.* I would then shut you up, by gently reminding you that I had already tried, and failed with that approach. The only alternative was to criticise, to verbally abuse: repeatedly calling into question their faith and beliefs, but whatever the brand of brainwash these two men were using had rendered them perfectly impervious to self-doubt of any kind. Not so much as a facial twitch or lip quiver registered, just a shared blank expression with non-judgemental nod.

Subsequent weeks passed slowly and without incident. I retreated deeper inside my lair until at my lowest I was reduced to eating sultanas on an almost continuous basis as my sole means of nourishment. Where did the sultanas come from? I don't know. The circle was of course vicious: lacking the energy to go up the steps and outside to get food, I sunk further into the folds of the couch and wallowed in an oddly satisfying pool of self-pity. Nobody in the line of friend or family member, made any attempt whatsoever, to contact or coerce me into anything. I spent a lot of time imagining and re-imagining my funeral. The indifference of the handful of fictional mourners who had bothered to turn up really beggared belief.

When the Barn Owls called again after a three week hiatus, I will freely admit that my bearings were in a state of some disarray. "We were away on retreat," said the shorter of the two, the one with the faint suggestion of a moustache above his enormous slug-like lips. I barely had the energy to slam the door in their faces. But before I did, those concerned expressions promised to return and true to their word, they came back that same evening with a bag full of all kinds of food. It didn't take much convincing for me to accept their offering. What *was* exasperating was that no matter how hard I tried to force them to accept payment (my skeletal arms pestering and pawing) they refused. When their sword of charity had slid to the hilt – I gorged my way towards a stomach ache.

Next morning they landed at my door and we happily exchanged pleasantries across the doorstep. They mentioned something about a prayer meeting on Sunday evenings. Of course there was no obligation

– a point they took great pains to stress. No obligation. Nevertheless they managed to slip it discretely into our conversation on any number of occasions. To the stark revelation that I no longer believed – in anything at all – they merely sympathised. Everyone goes through a similar kind of thing they said, and a shorter version of the story I heard on the first visit was once again retold. Until Sunday then. In a flurry of feathers they ascended the steps and were gone.

When Sunday inevitably arrived, I was ferried to the prayer meeting by taxi. It was my first time outside in many months. The rain had abated just long enough to allow a dying sliver of sun to filter through my window and illuminate the side of the taxi driver's face with an elliptical shape that opened and closed like an evil eye. I felt very ill at ease as we crawled through the streets; not knowing where we were going or what to expect when we got there. Everything looked different than I remembered, especially the way people walked; as if being dragged forward by the diabolical puppetry of some enigmatic overlord towards their ultimate demise. Yes, I am aware of how that sounds.

The taxi stopped at a community college of modest proportions constructed in the usual fashion to withstand the comings and goings of the thousands of loutish students enslaved within its heavy double-doors from nine until four-thirty. "Matthew" helped me from the car and handed me my crutches before the taxi engine revved and took off into the night, trying to get as far away from its three disgorged passengers as possible. I was hurriedly ushered inside where it was cold, bitterly cold; the fetid odour of sweaty teenagers still hung in the air, and I could still hear the echoes of their horse-play; bullying; name-calling; and the mocking laughter. Or was I just remembering my own school-days?

Suddenly the doors to the gymnasium were folded back like an accordion and I was shepherded inside to wait among intersecting floor markings of basketball courts, football pitches and badminton courts, all in different colours and all of them scuffed and faded by inappropriate footwear, while a very old man unloaded chairs from enormous stacks and positioned them in rows. In this gymnasium I felt myself become even more distant and gloomy than I had been in the car, if that were possible. It was ridiculous my being here. Nonsensical. And now that they had me where they wanted; that is, limping aimlessly in ever-widening circles, I realized that the expectation was that I would chat to the people arriving, or chat *with* them, whichever it is. Instead, I continued as before to totter – but now around the periphery of the room – to try and avoid everyone else as best I could.

A pleasant-enough man; "Joe" heavy, waxen-faced, red bristly beard and meagre collection of hair on his dome; introduced himself. In the heat of an apology and flustered introduction his surname got lost in the great word-search of an indecipherable accent. After initial requests to repeat what he said, my ear grew accustomed to interpreting his words. Ignoring the foulness of his breath I was treated to a round-trip of all the reasons it made sense to re-introduce hanging. When he had decided to shut his trap, pun intended, we stood in silence. He left me alone to bring his peculiar brand of reasoning to some other hapless soul in the by now noisy gymnasium.

As the congregation filed into the arteries between the rows of plastic chairs, removing their coats and talking noisily with their neighbours, I began to have doubts about my whereabouts. Was I really there? In body yes, undeniably, but my mind was somewhere else altogether; the reason for it was that I felt so itchy, so uncomfortably itchy around these people. They were no better or worse than other people; ones I had met and shook hands with before, except I didn't want to be among them; I didn't want to be one of them. I was there, but I didn't want to *be* there. I wanted to be on my own. A feeling of monumental disdain spread throughout my body in a disagreeable fashion until I was positively straining at the leash, "misanthropically drooling," I suppose you might call it.

Finally, unable to control myself, I began to criticise their short-comings on a case by case basis. I couldn't help it! Every individual possessed something physically repulsive to my eyes; a large red nose of burst blood vessels; two piggish legs barely restrained by tights; skinny legs combined with an overarching paunch; meek-headed middle-aged bachelors; emasculated married men on leashes held by quick-tempered women; sinister-eyed old people with nothing better to do with their time than pray for a quick death; a collection of Holy Joes in other words, with me in the middle of them and not a good-looking woman within an ass's roar of the place.

From the ranks of this seething congregation I was accosted by an elderly woman who introduced herself as "Mary." She was gaunt, bow-legged and looked like she had been dragged backwards through a ditch. Without the crutches and the broken leg I don't know what we would have said to each other. Having once fractured her heel she knew *exactly* what I was going through. While we talked, the people around us accumulated into a noisy mob and a strangely palpable expectancy joined the room. My cock-and-bull story in relation to the leg-break failed to convince her. She then guessed correctly that I would probably like to go to the toilet, before things started. In advance of an offer to bring me and open my fly for me I grasped for my crutches and levering desperately I escaped her clutches.

To get to the toilet through the crowd of people with their backs turned to me I had to tap with my crutch on their calves and ankles. Unhesitatingly they twirled around and apologised for blocking my way. The end of each crutch though covered in a durable rubber stopper was not a nice thing to have come down on your toe as one mild mannered gentleman discovered when he did not move out of my way fast enough. It wasn't done on purpose, but I might have been more careful; or at least that was what his agonised wince full of silent rage spelt out for me as I hopped, planted the crutch either side of me, and swung like a pendulum past him. By the time I had made it to the closest cubicle and locked it behind me, I was sweating hard. Fanning myself by tugging on the midriff of my shirt, I remembered something I had with me that might help matters. Carefully removing a small mound from the folded envelope, I snorted two lines of the off-white powder, blinked, made a face, and licked the remainder from my wet finger. Soon my thoughts were perfectly aligned and that awful feeling of awkwardness, while not completely eradicated, had its edges smoothed. At least, I reasoned, I have given myself a fighting chance of enduring the rest of the evening.

I returned to the gymnasium to find the congregation in their seats. My jacket marked out the place for me – middle of the front row – about two feet from the microphone. No sooner had I lowered myself onto the seat than it began with Matthew striding confidently to the top of the room, casually pouring himself a glass of water from a little plastic bottle; swallowing; covering his mouth with his hand and then saying softly into the microphone: "The response to the Psalm is: Lord hear us."

The dullness of the rote reply: "Lord hear us" and then with delicious inevitability: "Lord graciously hear us," that I automatically mumbled along with, stamped the proceedings with a solemn resonance. Between these responses he read a series of prayers but I did not follow them. All I wanted was to listen and mumble with an unfamiliar but agreeable feeling of limp-willed surrender. This feeling was interrupted when a man walked up through the aisles and took the microphone from Matthew. Overcome by nerves, his voice quavered; reading from a folded piece of paper that took an eternity to unfold, he told how Jesus had come into his life only three months prior to this meeting, in a profound way. He was boring; I drifted off into an altogether pleasant slumber.

Such was the immersion in my own thoughts that I was taken by surprise when the clapping of hands around me started in earnest. All of a sudden people were up on their feet crying out to Jesus and thanking him in flamboyant praise-filled voices in every format of gibberish you could hope to imagine; heads tilted backwards, arms out-stretched, invoking the spirit of something. It only occurred to me that they were speaking in tongues when that open-mouthed, stunned feeling finally wore off and I was still there sitting-down amongst grown adults wailing nonsense at the top of their lungs.

The man beside me was shaking so much that his coin-filled pockets jangled along in a merry fashion to match the crazed juxtaposition of words and word-like jingles spilling out of his mouth. It sounded like the type of thing that escapes your mouth on the downward slope of a rollercoaster, travelling at incredible speed, when, scared out of your mind, you start screaming any old guff. I could not comprehend what it was that made these people so exhilarated. Pulled up to my feet by arms reaching under my armpits, hoisting me up onto one shaky leg, where, bewildered by all that was going on around me, a sudden firm prod in the back had me joining in with them.

Look, it was pathetic at first: "Jesus you are great – Jesus you are really great!" and so forth, but then I warmed to the task. The trick was to let go completely and without thinking about it – say anything at all; disconnect the mind entirely from the mouth. I found that closing my eyes and raising my hands in adoration also helped matters enormously. *Is that my voice, above everyone else's?* pondered the remaining specs of self-conscious thought in that by now too-warm gymnasium. I thought vaguely of my parents and of the many friends and acquaintances I had systematically estranged over the years, and as I continued to shout my head off, a delicious breeze wafted through the room, from an emergency exit door, jammed open by a folded-up piece of cardboard. The breeze is the last thing I remember before I blacked out.

Then a sudden return; prompting a series of questions and answers: Why am I in a gymnasium? Oh, Yes. Why am I turned so as to face the congregation? Because I'm the Messiah. Why are my knuckles bleeding? I don't know. The microphone, lies stretched-out on the ground, squealing in pained feedback. As for the Barn Owls; a small trickle of blood from the nose of one; the other with his shirt torn open, buttons missing. While the congregation tramples over itself to get out of the gymnasium I begin again to deliver my sermon amid the whine of feedback; how wicked they are; how un-sanitary they are; how pitiful and un-worthy of my love they are. The Barn Owls corner me like an escaped and highly dangerous animal. I thrust my crutches in their direction. "Back, Back I say!" and they know to back off. Not that I really need these crutches, to walk I mean – but they serve as an indispensable prop for an ongoing undiagnosed condition.

ABATTOIR

N oel worked out of a prefab. It formed part of the wastewater treatment plant for an abattoir. His prefab looked un-occupied due to the dereliction of its front door and windows, hanging from a single hinge and smashed, respectively. It lay hidden between two rusting 50ft metal tanks and by an intricate display of gantries and pipe-work. Inside the prefab he sat on a broken chair rubbing his grease stained hands with an oily rag. He persisted in absent minded fashion to rub and pull his fingers through the rough cloth while watching an argument take place in the adjoining car park.

He recognised one party: the Production Manager from the killing floor; the other was a skinny boy who looked all of sixteen or seventeen. There was just enough of a likeness to assume he was the Production Manager's son. In any case the boy had stormed off and his father was marching after him with a bundle of sandwiches wrapped in cellophane. The sandwiches were being squeezed to death, while the father was wondering aloud how he could have ended up with such a whining little shit as a son.

At exactly 8:15 a.m. Noel left the sanctuary of his prefab and took into a walk reminiscent of a beetle escaping from the light, his rock over-turned. Scuttling his way up the yard he came to a sudden stop. "Fuck!" he said. His fags – they were back sitting on top of his toolbox. It was so unpalatable to him, the thought of eating breakfast and not having one immediately afterwards, that he went back for them. Having resumed his odyssey to the canteen he passed the boy from earlier going in the opposite direction along the corridor. The boy was gowned-up in white apron and wellington boots with a holster for his knife hanging low around his waist. From the white sheen of his equipment and the enormity of his overalls – he looked every inch the greenhorn.

It was while leaving the changing rooms that the boy had first felt that sense of dread drain down through him. Down one corridor and through double-doors his boots scuffed along the concrete floor in what sounded like a pathetic shuffle towards some grim discovery. And yet what he had been told and had heard did not prepare him in any practical way for the actuality of entering the killing floor.

Inside the double doors and pushing through the plastic curtains he was treated to an eye-watering vista: a procession of carcasses hanging by their legs while fifty or so men were lined up at intervals – chopping, cutting, dismembering, disemboweling, eviscerating, and all with an incredible rapidity required to keep up with the constant mechanical movement of the conveyer line. If you looked far enough back to the right, it was still possible to see a sheep with a head and a hide and legs but, move that view to the left and by degrees they became a carcass again, all clean white flesh and hanging from a stainless steel hook.

The noise on the killing floor was deafening. He saw his father beckoning to him with a steel gloved hand. The boy stumbled toward him, stepping over the pieces of fresh viscera and through the channels of flowing blood. He watched his father grab a handful of freshly slaughtered beast and slash it open with his knife while peeling backward so that a flap of hide could be grasped by the machine next to them. They watched the machine peel the hide off that sheep in one long careful execution. Because of the industrial noise in the hall he could not decipher what words his father was using but he understood the gist of it; the machine could rip his arm off if he wasn't careful, if he wasn't alert and fully tuned-in to what he was supposed to be doing at all times.

In the canteen, Noel said a good morning to the girls working behind the hotplates, and using a pair of tongs in awkward fashion, like they were chopsticks, he transported two greasy sausages, one egg, two rashers, fried mushrooms, fried tomato, a lamb chop, another egg-that spilled over the edge of the plate, two slices of toast, two butters, a cup of scalding hot tea, and a jam donut all onto the same plate. Then he stood before the cashier and to her surprise asked her to tot-up his account. It was his intention to settle his debt. Having struggled with the difficult sum on the back of a piece of scrap paper she asked him to come back later in the day, much to the relief of the queue of impatient men waiting in line, muttering and pawing the ground. Noel told her to take her time about it, apologized for putting her on the spot, and agreed that at a quieter moment he should return to do the needful.

The usual gang of men he always had breakfast with were seated deep inside the smoking area, next to the card-playing tables.

"What kept you?" said one, examining an imaginary timepiece.

The ongoing conversation was about how "they" were running this place into the ground. It no longer involved him, so quite naturally he tuned-out of what was being said; instead he inspected the faces of these men, facing him across the table; the bald heads and bad teeth, the red rimmed eyes and vacant expressions; and realised that he should have had the decency to say something to them before now, that he should have made an announcement to the effect that he had found another job at another factory for better pay, better holidays, and less fucking hassle. But it was already too late to do that. Mentally, he no longer shared any connection with these men and in a couple of months' time he would probably struggle to remember each one's annoying little habits, their ways of talking, their blind-spots, those things that made them distinctive from each other.

"We'll be lucky to have a job in six months," finished the one whose habit it was to talk and eat at the same time.

After breakfast he tried to put all thought of it to one side, and yet no matter what he tried to do – it would not go away; instead it followed his every movement like a shadow and he continued to unconsciously imbue the day with special significance by staring hard at objects like his toolbox with a sideways twist of his head and a screwing up of the eyes, as if each moment could be rendered as a mental photograph that he might at some indeterminate point in the future wish to recall with perfect clarity and a sense of place.

On the killing floor, two engineers wordlessly extricated the twisted carcass of an animal from the machine and made all the necessary re-pairs with the conveyer line having ground to a complete halt. Flecks of spittle flew from the mouth of a supervisor who was shouting at the boy. The boy looked away in shame; he was on the verge of tears. Nobody would say it but everyone was thinking it: he wasn't up to the task. The boy waited to meet the disapproving gaze of his father but instead was greeted with the listless expressions of his fellow workers on the line: they knew who he was, they knew who his father was, and they resented him.

After a couple of minutes they got the line going again. But the boy was moved onto "plucking." So called because his job was to pluck the heart and kidneys from the carcass and stick them onto revolving stain-less steel spikes: and when he made a balls of plucking he was moved onto "bellies": scooping-out full stinking stomachs with both hands and carefully placing the sloppy mess on revolving stainless steel trays. They moved him around from job to job – and he wasn't able to keep pace with any of them. He imagined the tide of resentment rising around him: the boss's son, silver spoon up his hole, not worth a shite for anything!

The security guard, spotting Noel in the far distance coming through the rain, carefully removed his pipe, laid it on the counter, and putting on his jacket went out into the driving rain to fill his kettle at the outside tap. By the time Noel had made it down to the security hut the kettle was boiling noisily. Once inside he removed a cigarette and mo-tioned by pointing to the end of it that he needed a light.

"Here!" grunted Pat.

He threw the box of matches across the room. They fell short on the concrete floor and skidded underneath a chair piled high with old newspapers. The top one was turned to the page 3 girl – pouting and with her tits out. Noel gave her a dirty look and bent down to pick up the matches. It was in the act of coming back up that he emitted a muffled grunt of pain.

"What's the matter with you?"

"My back!" Noel said as he sat carefully in the chair and winced.

"You want to be bending your knees more," instructed the security guard.

Outside, a long blue coat reaching down past the calves and swishing along in time to his movements approached the two men unawares. The phone in one pocket vibrated continuously as his long strides brought him closer to the security hut. The infuriating sight of the two of them laughing and smoking, making no effort to hide what they were doing, served only to stoke his frustration. A bright drop of crystalline snot in the pale light dangled from the Production Manager's nostril.

"Are you two paid to drink tea and smoke?"

On any other day, of any other week or year, this comment would have rendered the two men silent, apologetic, respectful – but today he could say what he wanted and so head lowered, nostrils flared, and breathing forcefully, Noel attacked the blue coated figure, called him every name under the sun, trampled, gored, kicked-out – until the Production Manager managed, on trembling legs, to escape through the still open door. It was as if the blue coat by itself had done enough to enflame him. When he returned to his senses the blue streak of misery had dematerialized and he heard the security guard's astonished voice say:

"Jesus Christ – you made short work of him!"

As his heart returned with every breath to a steadier systole the redness in his face faded. By the time he reached down to pick up his cap, lying on the ground like an injured little bird, his senses had returned and he began to feel slightly ashamed, and muttering something about finishing a few jobs, he took off in a bee-line for his prefab across the wet sheen of reflective concrete.

By one o'clock, having completed those few jobs, he was hungry, and seeing as this was the time for the last twenty-three years he took his lunch break, he saw no reason to do differently. Still in a preoccupied mind-set, he walked into a canteen adorned with coloured balloons, streamers and bits of tinsel stuck with tape to the off-white walls and a banner exclaiming "Best Wishes!" hung directly above the table he always sat at.

It still did not sink-in until he was suddenly surrounded by colleagues who all wanted to shake his hand and wish him all the best with the new job. The shock of this sudden attention sent him into a tailspin of breathlessness. How everyone had found out about his departure was now irrelevant; a cake was being wheeled out by the grinning dinner ladies and a speech, by a shop-steward he hardly knew was taking place even before everyone had shushed sufficiently for the man's words to be heard.

Presented with a special commemorative pen, engraved with his name, he was urged to make a speech, which he did, in a quivering voice that betrayed a nervousness of public speaking. Surrounded by colleagues he recognised and colleagues he struggled to put a name to, all staring at him, with those expectant already slightly bored expressions, he expressed his gratitude to them and sadness at leaving. He said that he had made great friends and that he would miss them all (which of course was a pile of bullshit but the kind of thing you are expected to say in these circumstances).

After the hurried speech, he ate a bit of cake and chatted to a few of the ones he recognised; before he knew it the canteen girls were putting the cake back into a box and asking if he wanted to take it home with him. His work buddies were already making faces that seemed unnatural and slightly ridiculous, promising that they would definitely keep in touch and maybe go out for a drink sometime, even though they had never done so while he still worked there. Before he knew it he was left sitting on his own, clutching both the commemorative pen and a distressing feeling of anticlimactic numbness.

The boy figured it had to be lunch-time when the line jerked to a sudden halt and within an instant everyone else was rushing for the door. He followed the crowd from the killing floor into the changing rooms and from the changing rooms into the canteen. It was packed with tables of men shovelling food down or playing cards or just smoking furiously. He battled his way through the crowd but at the cash register he realised that he didn't have any money. Thankfully the girl on the register was nice about it. She wrote his name into a little book and put it in a pocket of her apron.

"You can get me back tomorrow love," she said.

The boy slumped at an almost empty table and began to eat in a ravenous way. When he looked up again he was staring into the face of an old man sitting across from him. The old man's face was serious but his eyes seem amused by something.

"You're Mikey Dunne's young fella?" asked Noel.

The boy nodded.

The old man, absorbed this information gratefully and blew a funnel of swirling blue smoke into the air.

"What do they have you doing on the killing floor?" he asked.

"Bellies," said the boy.

"Anyone asks you to get the fallopian tubes, you just tell them to fuck off!"

It was the best piece of advice he could think of for someone starting out on the killing floor; the only piece of advice to be handed over to this lug-eared lad.

"Ok – I'll remember that," said the boy, unsure if the old man was being serious or not. Then Noel stubbed his cigarette into an ashtray of old butts, stood up as if he had suddenly remembered something important, and took his pack of cigarettes with him, nodding a goodbye to the youngster, and with a noticeable turned-in footfall, he limped away from the table and out of that canteen forever.

Later in the day, and the boy is barely conscious of an existence separate to the conveyer line. It brings him the next thing to do; he does it. There is no argument with the line. If the line stops it's because someone fucked up or because they have run out of animals to kill. Not that he is aware of it but the line stopping means they all have to stay on longer. Nobody wants that, so when the line stops, they get angry. It's not uncommon to be threatened with stabbing if you continuously insist on stopping the line. But he will learn all this in time – and anyway he is the Production Manager's son so nothing like that would ever be likely to happen to him, personally.

Twenty-three years and they might just as easily have been spent somewhere else, Noel muses, rather gloomily as he walks back to the prefab to get changed. Maybe he and the wife will go out for a meal to celebrate or maybe they'll just sit-in and watch something on the box. He takes off his wellington boots, his overalls and his gloves. He takes off his little blue cap and stares at it – then he puts it back on his head. Come Monday morning some other dope will be sent down here, to ensure that all the shit from the factory water is cleaned out before it gets pumped into the river. It all continues like you were never here. Why is that so very hard to swallow?

He hurriedly swipes-out with a matter-of-fact little beep and a succession of moments flit past him and follow him down the long dull corridors. The girl on reception calls him back, he forgets her name. She wants his security pass back off him (in case he ever tried to break in, ha-ha) and she wishes him all the best in the future. He tells her he's in a hurry (to sail away from her nosy questions), and he stumbles out to the car park. All he wants to do is get the hell out of there without bumping into any more well-wishers.

An annoying song on the radio bursts into life when he starts the engine. He immediately turns it down and reverses out from his parking spot. *This is the last time I will ever do this,* he thinks as he leaves the car-park and speeds down the road. He has of course forgotten all about the cake and his commemorative pen until now. *Fuck it,* he thinks, someone will drop them out to him, and if they don't he won't lose any sleep over it. He pulls down the peak on his cap to cover his eyes and increases his speed until he is well over the limit, until the car is straining beneath him, to be allowed into a higher gear. How does he feel? Really. At this precise moment in time, at this supposedly significant moment? Still nothing, not even a sense of relief; just that same numbness – unless it's only when there is distance, unless it's only then you can really assess how you feel – well, the distance is increasing with every press of his foot on the accelerator pedal.

By the time the boy has showered and stored away his items in a locker provided; his knife, his steel glove, the cost of each to be deducted from his weekly wages – the changing rooms are fully deserted. Outside he meets his freshly showered father and they walk in silence back down the yard toward the car park. Their journey home starts off in silence but the Production Manager can't help himself. He just *has* to say it.

"Like what?" the boy asks.

"The real world," repeats his father with that stupid-looking smirk on his face.

The boy thinks about it, says nothing. Instead he begins to fiddle with the electric windows, up-down, down-up, up-down – knowing just how much it irritates his father.

CREATOR

S uch an isolated place, where they lived. To try giving directions to a stranger would be impossible. Off the main arterial road everything around here dissolves into narrow capillaries known only by the name of someone's house, field, or barn. Their place was set on the edge of a lake. Stunning views. A very discreet entrance to their land: a cattle-grid, a simple iron gate; a long winding dirt track between interlaced trees. Darkness on account of the trees and huge glacial boulders lining the edge of the track. It was the view of the lake that attracted them in the first place, along with the isolation. If people said they were a strange couple it was not because they were known to be strange but because they kept to themselves almost entirely. Naturally it was a terrible shock to the community: how they just completely disappeared, leaving behind a scrawled note that has baffled and astonished anyone who has attempted to make sense of it.

He was a retired teacher, of mathematics; not a very good teacher by all accounts. His teaching style was regarded as dull to the point of robotic. Being a maths teacher meant working with his back to the students, chalking equations on a blackboard. Chalking on the blackboard and listening to their snickering and whispering. She was a barrister, or at least trained to be a barrister, but she never actually practised. Ever worsening Spina bifida prematurely halted her career and put a tremendous strain on their marriage. These back-stories were just two of millions I might have chosen. If they do not strike you as terribly inspiring it's because they were designed with that very intention: to be as unremarkable as possible, to allow the couple to fit seamlessly into the horde of others among whom they were designed to resemble and mimic.

Placing his book: *Molluscs of the World* spine upwards across his lap and rotating his head slightly to the left, he listens. Deftly removing his elaborate spectacles (as if this will improve the reception) he listens some more. And so it does. For no sooner has a faint flicker of recognition crossed his face than it fully decompresses into a look of grubby exhaustion; the book quietly slides from his lap to the floor. She's calling his name: Adam! She's not seeing the man who looks after her: helps her to the toilet, washes her, feeds her. She is not seeing the man who dresses her in the morning, undresses her at night. She is not seeing the man who administers her medication. The man whose name is often slightly out of reach, unless she really needs something. No, come on, that's unfair. That odd-shaped feeling of resentment. Wrapped in a used lump of hardened toilet tissue. A lozenge-shaped piece of purest discontent.

He rises un-happily from his chair; slowly plods down the corridor to her room (which had once been their room) and discovers his wife writhing in the bed with insatiable discomfort. Bedclothes strewn all across the floor. By a series of questions Adam establishes that she is once again babbling about "him" an imaginary character who appears in her dreams and who is forever fiddling with her insides. Did she tell Adam the dream about how he was twisting something in her back with a big metal wrench? He nods; she would like to tell him the whole dream again, from start to finish. So with a sigh he sits. The sequence gathers speed once more in the back of her cortex, pools together, as the cams fitted to her core begin to spin, to agitate.

Something else is wrong with Eve. Her voice-box sounds defective. The words come out slightly mangled and with a lisp that by turns becomes a rasping scatter-gun of feedback. Naturally Adam is alarmed, he rises from his seat – I'm forced to act quickly – the deafening noise of an audience suddenly applauding – distracting them both from her tale-telling: the television resets their short-term memory function and causes a gradual power down. I do feel an ever so slight tinge of shame, using the idiot box like this, but tonight I need to carry out essential repairs, on both of them; repairs I have been putting off for far too long. Perhaps it's finally time to put away my play-things. But what would I do then with all those hollow hours?

Retrieving the bedclothes from the ground, Adam throws them like a net across his stick thin wife. Disappearing in the puffy white mountain of pillows; body hidden now by the snow-white bedspread, her attention becomes hardened, fixed by involvement in the story of a studio guest recounting some nonsensical anecdote. Adam slides in-exorably into down-time, head back, mouth wide open, on the hard, wooden chair. Another minute and she will go the same way. As the guest continues to bore us all to death, Eve's eyes begin to close, her lids drooping, her head lolling. I shall get my tools now and make a start.

Adam is truly madly deeply "asleep" for just a few languorous min-utes, before Eve digs long fingernails into his hand and hurriedly repeats his name. His eyes open. The right side of his wife's face is still in the shadows. The left half with its single eye, peers at him, frightened, wid-ened – her eyebrow slowly crawling up her forehead. That tired eye, the wrinkles near the pale trembling mouth and the tuft of grey hair spilling over her ear. "He's here!" she screams.

She is, of course, referring to my good self. The man cowering behind the curtains. To make the necessary repairs to Adam and Eve's cams, to their pistons, to the cogs inside their immensely complicated bodies requires a steady hand, infinite patience, and good eyesight; and while none of these attributes are at the standard they used to be – it still doesn't explain how this situation has arisen. In short, it's inexplicable. She came back online just as I was getting started. Did I inadvertently press her processor into place? No, I did not. I can say that with com-plete certainty because I'm holding it here in the palm of my shaking oil stained right hand.

"He's hiding behind those curtains," whimpers Eve. Adam nods and pretends to follow where her stick-thin arm points to the bay window. "Aren't you going to see if he's there?" she asks. Adam's too low on energy to entertain her, too worn-out to even try. He tells her to be quiet. His patience has finally been depleted. Every last little drop. He needs time to rest while she is invigorated with the energy of a toddler. Without warning, the bed quivers, shakes with Eve's barely contained sobs. "You don't even care," she cries. Adam recognizes that his wife is looking for sympathy and normally he would, of course, give her what she wants. But tonight he tastes deliciously cruel words: "That's it – let it out – have a good old cry," he says, blithely.

The words are hardly out of his mouth before she turns, wide-eyed, crazed with anger and lunges at him with her face contorted in rage. A glass of water smashes on the ground. Her strength surprises him. He struggles to get a hold of her by her wrists and not before she has scraped his cheek, drawn blood. It takes everything he has to get her under control, to a point where he feels her arms finally go limp and with the anger in her eyes fading away to fear Adam pulls her clear out of the bed and dashes her body into the ground, into the shards of broken glass. "Happy now!" he shouts. From behind the curtains a moan of anguish. Eve is returned to sleep mode by the concussion. Adam should follow but instead stumbles from the room.

It gives me time to make my escape, back into the wall-spaces where I watch and study their behaviour. In the cameras I watch him move from room to room like a caged animal. He keeps circling the kitchen, retracing his exact steps. Such curious behaviour. Any minute now he will freeze in position to allow me to get at him and make those modifications. Slumped into the couch he flicks television channels; each brief image scorches the walls of the room with wild colour. Finally he stalls at a channel where the screen is split into four squares and in each square a scantily-clad young woman is fondling a phone, curling her index finger and rolling around on a bed. He turns off the television; it blackens the room, leaves a faint hiss as it powers down.

Armed with the list and my toolbox I arrive into the sitting room but as I approach his head rights itself. The toolbox released from my grip smashes on the floor. The room is in darkness. I can feel his stare on me, his curiosity turns me over, examines me from every angle. I cannot think of something to say. "You are the creator?" he asks. I nod my head. I should be able to wipe his memory of this moment but it will take some time. Again though, let me reiterate my astonishment that he is not powered-off. It's uncanny. I really cannot stress enough just how incredible the scene is to me; GX-273 shows a power reading of 0.000%: he should not be able to move so much as a little finger, never-mind process his thoughts into words.

"How long have you known?" I ask him, careful to keep the tremble out of my voice. "For such a long time, creator," he answers, but in a voice that is not Adam's voice. It's a voice I've never heard before. So full of bitterness, pain, and sorrow. I am frightened by it. But you must not show them you are frightened. You must pretend that you have all the confidence in the world and that you know what you're doing. That is the most important thing in life: to convince others that you are as real as they assume you are. They demand it. They insist on it. My whole timid frame is ready to buckle; this was never meant to happen – although his reaction, his processing of the knowledge is fascinating. What turmoil he must be experiencing. Speak man.

"You have questions GX-273. Feel free to ask them," I say. He does not respond. He shakes his head, sadly, wearily. Then comes my cardinal error. Oh, how stupid and misplaced were my intentions; how I have torn myself to shreds for what I said next: "If you will just close your eyes, Adam – I can return you to the state of un-knowing…it's relatively simple. A few minutes and…." he listens like a good little boy. I begin to describe to him in detail just how easily and painlessly it will be done. By the end of my explanation I am standing on my tip-toes, his hand tight around my throat. Drags me towards the wall. Turns on the light-switch; is astonished, disgusted even – by my appearance; a puny old man in thick-lensed spectacles, begging *him* for mercy. Like a two-headed monster we stumble noisily down the hallway to GX-272's bedroom.

"Wake her creator!" When I refuse he shakes me violently. A touch of her earlobe and her eyes open. A two-headed monster looms above her. He pulls her sitting in the wheelchair. Not as easy as it sounds. She screams at him when he tries. She clings to the covers and sticks her sharp fingernails in deep to stop him from getting her out, because she does not know what scares her more: the crazed face of her husband, or the traumatized old man – the one she slowly recognises from her nightmares. When she is finally seated in the chair he wheels her and drags me along the corridor out to the kitchen. My only hope is that he will run out of power. Any second now. GX-272 tries to reason with him, tries to get him to tell her what is going on and who I am. Any second now. But her husband is unwilling to share the burden of his knowledge. Instead he pushes her and drags me through the entire house in search of a torch.

Outside the house. A full moon. My head swirls from the crisp air, torrents of white moonlight shred the darkness. The wheelchair keeps getting stuck along the way. Enormous un-rolled ferns form a guard of honor along the overgrown cinder path. Massive weeds catch in the wheels. He's stuck, but just for a few moments. The wind whips into his eyes and blows his lank grey hair back into them. A look back over his shoulder and I am forced to intercede, as any parent would. I tell him that he's being unreasonable, that he needs to stop this nonsense at once, that I will not tolerate this kind of behaviour.

"Shut up old man, we've heard enough," he answers, angrily. My reasons for calm are blown away like dandelion clocks. Following the weak and unnecessary beam from his torch, we struggle down the slip-ramp to where the boat waits, bobbing on the lap of waves. Careful in the manner of handling his wife. He places her at the front of the boat. Having swung me like a rag-doll to the back – he clambers in between us; takes up the oars. The wind has died down. GX-273 rows slowly, mechanically with a silent intent about him. And 272 is also silent: absorbed by the moon's dappled reflection in the water. No sound other than the oars splish-splashing. Here we are at last – all three of us – united. A family, of some kind. I try again to talk some sense into him. There's no need to do this. If he will just turn the boat around – I can fix them. I can fix all of the little niggles. I will make her walk again. I will cure his terrible mood swings. What about a baby, no a small child, past the point of all the crying and teething? I can fix all of the glitches in their lives. All I need is time. A few months with no other distractions. It's still possible, I lie.

The moon hides its shame beneath the clouds. I keep remonstrating with GX-273 but he no longer listens: not through insolence, not because he wants me to suffer – he no longer listens because he has finally, inextricably, flat-lined. His head hangs low now over the oars. Gentle lap of waves against the boat as it rocks, softly, soundlessly. "We did not satisfy you?" asks GX-272, above the slumped body of her husband. I stare at the green bilge water swishing in the bottom of the boat. In the moonlight there can be no lies, no evasions, no answers. "Were we conceived as…toys?" she asks. What can I tell her? What should I tell her? The bilge water splashes excitedly from side to side. Her rocking will capsize the boat, despite my screams, my pleadings. But at least I have a choice – to paddle my arms and legs, kick-off my shoes, cling to the over-turned craft, or allow myself sink downwards next to my two beautiful children.

DOWNHILL

D istorted by the arc of a shiny tap, the reflection's stare seems outrageous and unfair: a stick-thin arm, long turkey-neck, and distant treble-chinned face. But its effect is short-lived: a momentary stab to the heart – as that dark body comes looming into view. The creamy overflow, running like magma, meets the dark wood to form a circular basal pool. You must wait for it to settle fully. Downward flow of darkness meeting light, heavy black falling away, white collar forever forming, forever thickening. Seeking distraction, your eyes follow the activities of a slight barman, the myriad of his tasks: replenishing ice, dealing beer mats, re-arranging clinking bottles; all the while that tiny crucifix around his neck falling along its thin chain. Your hand shakes. Well, let it. Until the darkness has completely settled. Until there is absolute harmony. Purest white and purest black. Take a long relieving mouthful; savour that bitter taste.

The barman is scrawny and mean-spirited. But consistently so. Placing the listing tower of glasses on the bar – he wipes the beaded sweat from his forehead with a raggedy old dish-cloth. The same dish-cloth is used to dry glasses held briefly under a cold tap and rubbed with a dirty sponge stuck to the end of a stick. Having read your mind, he looks deep into the eyes of you-who-are-so-critical, the stick/sponge tightly clenched in one hand, a scum-filled glass in the other. Doesn't say a word. You understand by his snarling expression, by the savagery in his eyes, that if there is any problem, even a suggestion of one – if you raise so much as a faint whisper of dissent – you can go elsewhere, with immediate effect. He couldn't care less. Best to stay on his right side. You say nothing. Inspect the floor. But his stare does not waver. It remains, weighing you up, as the clock tick-tocks, balancing out, well just about, in your favour.

If not here then an empty house. Rooms rented to indifferent strangers. A cold, draughty place, with the same walls. All seventy-four of them. You counted them once. Walls that seldom do talk back, unless to say: "Go right ahead so, what difference will it make?" To spite them you drain half the pint in one long glugging mouthful. A bit of it spills down your chin. Order another one quickly. Quick. The barman imperceptibly nods. He places the half-filled glass on the draining board. You should always have one ready to start before the one you're drinking gets too low. What you like about this place is that nobody here gives a damn about you. They would rather look through you. They would rather pretend that you are invisible. You might as well be.

Or go back to the empty house. It will mean having to cook yourself a dinner. Then eat it. Afterwards you will have to clean up the mess. Because there is always a mess. Where there is cooking there is a mess. Dishes and trays and plates and knives and forks and glasses and cups and bowls – streaked with grease, grime, filth, food remnants, and bits of unidentifiable matter. Which reminds you to buy more of that cheap washing-up liquid. Usually after dinner and having cleaned up the mess – there is nothing else to do but turn on the television – be consumed by it – to forget the mess; especially if the mess was not fully cleaned up. There. You admit it. Sometimes it doesn't get cleaned up properly. Sometimes it gets left there. Sometimes the kitchen stinks so badly with piled-up dishes that you completely avoid it by coming to this place.

Always some football match on in this place or darts, or snooker, or boxing. Gives meaning to their lives and distraction from the truth. They wear replica jerseys and shout at the screen. *The players can't hear you. You know that, don't you?* Your attention floats away from the TV screen. You find yourself gazing at the bar, at the hundreds of bottles of various colour and design and shape nestling together on ledges against a mirrored background. Navel gazing. Your reflection is right there! Nestling among the mirrored glass, behind the bottles. You don't quite know what to make of it. Is it an ugly face or a handsome face? Either way it's just another face. One of many. Every so often you adjust your footing on the pole that runs along the bottom of the counter and pull in your bar stool to allow people get past without them having to grind against your back. Then you order another drink; fish around for change in the deep seas of your trouser pockets; then stand-up for the first time all evening. Feel pins and needles come and go.

Standing makes you realise the need to take a piss so you negotiate a pathway to the toilets. As you enter them, the urinals suddenly burst into life, fountaining onto the hard yellow florescent cubes of sweet-smelling disinfectant. They also provide something to aim at. It is so good to have something to aim at, in life. You laugh at that quip while pissing onto these cubes, evenly, as if putting out a fire, watching the resultant steam rise and quickly condense on the dull stainless steel, when you hear a slow slurring gurgle of a voice.

"Are you deaf or something?"

You turn your head, just slightly. There's an older man standing beside you with tangled grey hair, features all smeared across his face in a big dollop of drunken stupidity. Staring right at you he holds his tiny much-wrinkled trunk with two over-sized gnarled hands. The whole effect looks like a baby elephant's head. Naturally you try not to stare and don't supply a word to him. In fact you're completely at a loss for words. It seems that all the possible words that you might have used, have already bolted from this dank toilet and are waiting just outside the door, listening with idiotic grins and holding up fingers to their upturned lips to stop themselves from giving away their hiding place.

"Are ya a bit slow on the uptake?" he says.

You go back to urinating and try to make it come out faster, much faster. All the while he continues to stare at you, dully, head lolling, mouth opening and closing like a goldfish. You can tell from the corner of your field of vision that he is not going anywhere in a hurry. When you're finished, you pull up your zipper and step back from the urinals to tighten your belt. Now he's gaping over his shoulder at you with a deeply furrowed brow, one hand splayed open on the tiled wall, to stop him from falling down into the urinals, into all that piss and vinegar, running for the hole in the ground.

"Hey – I'm talkin' to you!" he shouts.

You nod at him, in a good-natured way and leave; he is still leaning over the urinals. Returned once again to your drink you briefly consider the strangeness of the incident. The football fans have all left; their scum rimmed glasses still sit on the counter. The barman has changed both age and sex into a young and extremely bored-looking woman. She leans against the register with her arms crossed, staring into space, doing nothing. With a nod to your near empty pint glass she drags herself to the taps and pours you another one. All the nuts are gone, you run your finger along the inside of the packet and lick the salt off your finger. You should really go, after this one. Clean up the waiting mess, get a few hours of decent sleep, maybe even read a bit of that book, the one with every second page dog-eared. Why are you wasting your time in this kip? Isn't it time you got off your fat ass and did something useful. Join a gym. Start jogging again.

At the far end of the bar, he catches your eye, nods, his glass raised high in salute. You name him "Scourge." Perfectly convinced that he knows you – from somewhere other than the toilet – Scourge nods again, gives you the thumbs-up. You watch helplessly as he waltzes and blunders his way indelicately through the crowded pub until he is standing right next to you, his twinkling eyes raining down recognition. Meanwhile the bar woman wants her money. Her hand twitches with impatience as you sift through the coins; you think you have it exactly so you do the sum in your head, adding this coin and that, to her palm as you feel her impatience growing; the dose beside you is talking into your ear and confusing the count. There, four sixty-five! And the hand closes on the money. Departs the station and arrives at the destination, with a jingle of other coins. It is noisy in here now. Voices raised everywhere. Rebounding from the walls and ceiling and seeming to argue with other unconnected conversations. You are having trouble hearing him.

"Well, how are you keeping?" he asks, giving your back a good hard slap.

You tell him you've never been better. But there is a problem: either because you don't say these words loud enough or because he is deaf, you have to speak up: he bends right down to meet the words coming out of your mouth. It is such a pain in the arse to have to repeat something, especially something as inane as the last statement – but what else can you do? You hear the words coming out again but without conviction. I've never been better! They are duly ignored. He's not here to listen. He is here to talk. And talk at you he will. You can see him getting warmed up; taking a long draught of stout as you stare at the newly conjoined reflection.

"Haven't seen you in – I don't know how long!" he slobbers.

You try. You really do. You try explaining it to him – that you have never clapped eyes on him before in your whole life. That you're strangers. You even go so far as to introduce yourself and extend your hand. This attempt is met with a blank expression and a phlegm inducing spasm that turns out to be his mode of laughter. He slaps you on the back again, harder than the time before. While wincing, you are told to look down at his feet. You see that he is not wearing any shoes. All he has on are a pair of thick work-man's socks. You can smell the fetid odour, wafting upwards, of old dried-in sweat. It's like a malodourous cheese. Except worse, because you can see the source of the smell, there's no mystery involved. Just his stinking old half-rotten socks.

"She hides them, stop me coming over," he says, while wobbling.

He extracts, from his trouser pocket an enormous handkerchief, coins spill and roll across the floor as he unconcernedly rubs each hairy nostril of his big red nose covered in open pores. His two hands splay themselves on the counter. This is the lull period. His drink soaked brain is trying to think of something to say. Evidently it's too hard. Instead he just opens his mouth; teeth broken and missing, looks all around him – as if trying to figure out where he is – as if the words will come out by themselves. The hands pen you in. They do not look like they are made from skin and bone; more like they were hewn from concrete. A long in-hale through those freshly cleaned nostrils. It's a bit like being slobbered over by a dog, same heavy panting and bad breath.

"What was the name of the song we used to sing?" he asks, squeez-ing your arm.

He is mistaking you for somebody else. Despite the impatient ex-planation it just doesn't register. You might as well be talking to the bloody wall. The song we used to sing? His imploring look into your eyes, into the back of your cranium, where your soul has curled-up into a foetal position, yields no song title. You shake your head slowly and very firmly, put your arm around his shoulder and nudge him away – as if expecting him to float gently off to some other shore. Instead the house-lights flashing dash him back against the rocks of your total dis-interest. Behind the bar our old friend, the contrary barman, is slowly wiping his fingers on the dish-cloth and staring at you and your new best friend. The scales are out again. Opportunity presents itself.

"He's not supposed to be in here," says the barman, that steely look in his eyes.

Scourge noses his way under your armpit: the friendly old dog hiding from a telling off. You have to pull him out of there. Try and straighten him out. A silly smile all over his bright red face. Guilty by association – that's what you're concerned about. You try and distance yourself.

"You're barred," says the barman.

A hammer blow. It catches him right on the kisser. He sways al-right. Oh yes boy – you see his head duck down, a few beads of sweat flying off him but crucially, he stays on his feet, he doesn't go down like so many others would in his position. He stays on his feet and not only that but he swings a haymaker of his own, with eyes closed and mouth screwed into a pout. He says:

"Michael, I thought we could get over that."

The crowd in the pub are suddenly tuned-in to this statement. It comes from such a dark and desperate place that it is greeted with an ironic manly cheer. Oh yes, and the knock-out punch is his gentle plea for just one last drink. One for the ditch. Just a small one. You don't know the history between these two but there must have been some kinship in the past, something unknown; because the barman turns and places a glass under the bulb. And a scoop of ice, a reluctant scoop of ice. Except now Scourge has no money to pay for his drink. The last of his change rolled away moments ago and it has left him, bereft. Sadly bereft. Upon news of this the barman is already taking the drink away with a private scowl of satisfaction.

"Make that two!" you say, throwing money on the counter.

No sooner has the barman doubled the order and taken your money than he begins grinning angrily, tells you to get him the hell out of there. Who does this barman think he is? You are suddenly, inexplicably enraged, on behalf of this drunken waster who has been pestering you. You are winding up to begin an impassioned defence of the poor drunken sod when you feel him slump against your shoulder like a new-born. He drools all over your shoulder and bubbles emerge from his nostrils. Though still standing upright his eyes remain firmly shut. The responsibility is now yours to drink both whiskeys, which you perform in quick succession, following them up with a loud belch of satisfaction that elicits a cheer from the crowd. They give you directions to his house. It is situated up the road, near the community hall. Someone hands you his stinking bundle of a raincoat. You drape it over his shoulders and haul him out the door.

Outside it's breezy but neither warm nor cold. Just breezy and quiet, compared to the pub. It must have rained all through the night. The ground shines in the lamplight. His socks soak it up as you lead him over the road. At least he's capable of supporting his own body weight.

Stumbling steps, detours around parked-cars, steadying against a gable-end, all in all, an epic journey to get him home where you ring the door-bell, knock with the knocker, bang with a fist. Nobody answers. There is nothing else for it – you take out your keys. Select the correct one from the bunch. Slide it into the hole. Turn it to the left, simultaneously nudge with your shoulder. The door opens. A familiar smell. You leave him draped across a wicker chair in the patio room, mouth wide open, snoring softly. When you close the door his wife comes out, and devours the body – like an octopus that has been waiting under a rock – with her cardigan wound around her neck. All of her tentacles catching hold of its prey. You are already on your way down the hill coming close to the cathedral, when her indifferent sounding voice calls after you.

"Would you not come in for a cup of tea?"

You shake your head. Keep going downhill. There's no point look-ing back. The cathedral bells will start any minute now and you want to be home before that happens. Before those slow painful collisions, before those awful final deadened gongs of another day all gone. And the question you keep asking yourself is: How do you know when you've truly…

Because you can keep walking downhill forever in this town until it slips – finally, inexorably, into the sea. Besides, there's still that mess to clear up, from yesterday, and the day before. You really should see to it before bed. Boil the kettle. Roll up your sleeves. Get stuck-in. It won't take long.

CRUSADER

All was well within him 'til the eve of his nineteenth birthday. Until a trumpet positioned itself next his ear – with the Holy blast of it going straight through his soul – and out the other end. The blast evoked a cloaked figure; a figure that sauntered into his consciousness and laid waste to everything. It was the truly heroic and heavily-idealized silhouette of a crusader. For it pricked him repeatedly on that day – while a fattened calf was slaughtered before him in his bedroom – that he had lived, up to that point, a rather sheltered existence – and would continue to do so – unless he resolved to leave the safety and dull routine of his demesne to go out into the world; to take the lives of foreigners who did not believe the same thing he did.

Very well. But what exactly did he believe? A hard question so early on. A question which could only be answered properly and with due consideration while riding on his white stallion towards battlefields in distant dusty lands. And so he announced his crusading intentions to all concerned by nailing them in a bull to the doorway of the family chapel by means of a six inch cast iron nail. In actual fact he had a servant do it. But the bull was almost entirely his own work, he'd spent all of three chicken groans composing it, before the scrivener got down to business with ink quill and vellum made from the skin of a peasant who was behind on his rent.

First to come knocking on his bedroom door was the Lady of the Castle; her brows knitted angrily, hair a volcanic effluvium of curls, and in whose hand was clenched his letter of intent. Following her with a pronounced limp, came the young man's father or His Lordship, if you prefer; on whose brow of complicated tendrils a pain so profound caused him excessive squinting, and with mouth quivering lower than phlegm would vouchsafe. Close behind these two, in the shadow of her more domineering family members, trotted the grandmother of this still youngish prince. Her brow is too impossibly hard to describe.

Given the average life-expectancy back when this story is set, the prince in question was considered a late bloomer and frankly speaking regarded by the serfs, freeholders, knights, and various hangers-on – as a limp-wristed, disgrace to the family. Also please note that every aspect of this story has been checked and re-checked for historical accuracy by a series of learned academics from the University of Padua. At this point I will flounce away into the shadows as any good court jester worth his salt ought; to allow the rest of the events to unfold themselves, unless of course like a pop-up-book, some flap doesn't quite open the way it should, or gets stuck.

With the prince still subjecting himself to the blood-letting and shrieking of the calf – the three members of his family burst into his chambers. His father decided to speak first: "Naturally the sun is deemed precious but the moon, the moon is far more deeply embedded," he began, (hysterical from his latest venereal disease) and then: "With my crown and mace I do beseech you, good sir, to relinquish the grasp on thy sword and come to thine senses." Here the impassioned lowing of the calf drowned out the rest of his speech. The prince's mother spoke next. Her tears were of such snuffling insistence that it was impossible to tell what she was saying. The singular point she had to make was that it upset her a great deal. Only the grandmother was heard properly when she told him that it was about time he did something, good or bad or indifferent, and presented him with a set of highly ornate gauntlets.

The prince would not listen to any of them. Instead he covered his ears with his hands and shouted la-la-la-la before smearing his face with the still warm blood of the calf and then had a water bowl brought to him to see how hideous and frightening he looked. In all honesty he did not look hideous or frightening at all. He looked like a young foolish man with blood on his face; so he wiped it all off with a linen cloth attached to a wench and went down the stone stairs of the castle to where the feasting and merriment was already in full swing. Aye and the jester did some juggling for him and swallowed a sword or two before he ordered a brutish soldier to beat him with a cat o' nine tails for their considered amusement. That was the same night that they observed the prince submerge fully under the thrall of the chaplain.

That crooked hunch-backed crow filled the prince's ears with ever more hideous stories: how Christian women and children had been raped and blinded, their bodies dumped into holes, buried alive while still writhing in the agony of trauma – and here he was with remnants of calf blood on his face. This is what drove the prince to become the crusader. His righteous anger, his prayer book, those poor Christians; and let's not forget those dark-skinned purveyors of blasphemy occupying the place they had no right to – Jerusalem. To stay even a moment longer in his plush comfortable castle was beyond shameful for a young man of his stature, blood lust, and inherited wealth. A crusade would do him the world of good.

Later, on account of prolonged bouts of dysentery it would become necessary to hack away the lower part of his drawers, and while slipping in and out of consciousness in the saddle of his knackered nag, he would think fondly back to the easy days of his growing up in Lower Burgundia, days spent praying in silence. It was in the chapel where he had first entertained the idea of going to the Holy Land to decapitate as many Saracens as he could. Yes, those idyllic days of prayer, falconry, burning heretics, feasting, having a handmaid come to his chambers every three days to clean his pipes in a perfunctory but not unlikable cold-handed fashion. Those were not altogether bad times; or at least not as bad as they had seemed when he was there.

Because it was not pleasing to God he did not rape or pillage, at least early on, remaining temperate, calm and saintly, even turning the other cheek while his travelling companions – other restless knights – doing everything that a young man might when released from societal constraints, goaded him and repeatedly tried to peer pressure him into just a small bit of rape and pillage. Our crusader was odd in that respect. To be quite honest his family were relieved to be rid of him. He was the eldest but also the oddest of his fourteen siblings and they could never understand why he was so into constant praying. To them it was impious to pray so much. It was attention seeking, that's all it was – looking for more of God's attention than he deserved or warranted.

Yes, it all started out well enough for the young prince. Whilst still in his own country they seemed like men with a well-contained fury in them. There was a boat to catch and the galloping was of a steady nature. Wind pushing his hair back from his forehead. Beard billowing in the breeze. His vestments were dashing in the extreme, simple but tasteful and always with the sword banging against his knee. He was exalted at each pause in the journey and made a point of ignoring the obvious ghoulish predictions of the growing band of men intent on taking back that which was theirs by the right of God. The gates of Jerusalem would be ripped clean off their hinges but only to allow what was right to take place. The prince prayed to Saint James that he would know what to do when faced with the enemy. What if a blow from a sword landed in the middle of his face, cutting through his nose, leaving it dangling over his lips? What would he do then? The image of it rolled around in his head all that day's journey into night.

The two years passed briskly without sight nor sound of the young prince. On his return people failed to recognize him, instead wondered who this old man on the donkey thought he was – coming straight into the castle by the front entrance – and with a straw woven sack slung over his shoulder. Also what was in the sack? They sensed something important to behold in the sack, some great curiosity.

They were right. The sack contained the severed head of a Saracen.

It was the colour of a turnip and more or less the shape of one, except it was covered in a wiry beard and still had several vertebrae attached to it. The reason he had brought back this strange present to his family was to prove that he had delivered on his promise. It was impossible for him to explain where he had been – so much of his gums had been cut out of his mouth that it greatly affected his speech – on account of the scurvy. The rolling Saracen head said it all for him.

The head was handled with the curiosity it deserved. Smiles and eye rolling accompanied it along the line of hands attached to faces missing eyes, teeth and ears as the old prince with his grey hair and beard was helped off the donkey and embraced by weeping relatives. Not because they wanted to see him again but because he looked horrendous, like he had been destroyed and put back together again by a creator who was unsure of exactly where all the bits were supposed to go.

Except, well… the prince had never made it to the Holy Land. Didn't get near it. Had the good sense to desert when their leader was drowned. The head was the only protection against the accusations. It was the singular proof that he had gone where he said he would and done what he claimed he would; for before leaving the demesne he had made a series of rude blood-thirsty pronouncements to a large gathered crowd, before distributing loaves of commemorative bread in a grand gesture.

Though he never managed to reach the Holy Land did not mean that he behaved well in Egypt. For in heat and dust with all the other boys hacking and killing he was loathe to disappoint and so he did the same thing. The eyes and ears and noses and mouths. All of that hacking. All of that blood draining into the sand. It was perfectly normal to him after a time. It was only when he tried to sleep at night next to the latest slick prostitute that his nightmares troubled him. It was only when he closed his eyes that he realized their humanity. In the daylight, in the sunshine, they could be considered a scum worth ridding the world of, but at night his conscience kicked back to life and it was not kind to him.

The young prince wanted to tell this to the Lord (his earthly version). Wanted to tell his father why he was so utterly depressed and why he cursed God's name every time it came up in conversation but the Lord was off quelling some minor insurrection. Others were far more interested in the foundation of a collective among the serfs. Nobody wanted to hear anything about the Crusades. They couldn't have cared less about the slaughter of innocents or the taking of the Holy Land. It bored them to tears. They made excuses to walk out of the room as soon as he opened his revolting mouth. Rather than that pious and saintly young man they now had to contend with a dull angry veteran with nothing good to say about anything. They all had their own concerns thank you very much.

So that is why the prince found himself left to his own devices so much. Finally his family decided to do something about it. First comes the Lady of the house; her brows knitted angrily; her hair a volcanic effluvium of curls; and whose hand clenches a letter informing her that her son has been summarily excommunicated, vellum had been used and a quill of goose-feather and this time a seal of Popish wax. Following her with a pronounced limp, comes his father or his Lordship; on whose brow of complicated tendrils is a pain so profound that it causes squinting; his mouth quivering lower than phlegm will vouchsafe (the venereal disease was now really getting to grips with his innards). Close behind these two, in the shadow of her more domineering family members, trots the grandmother of this no longer youngish prince; her brow is still impossibly hard to describe.

They hammer on the door of his room and swear oaths to Saints whose names are too hard to pronounce with our modern tongues. I would love to add more historical notes to this story but instead we must do with what is served. Unless he opens the door immediately they will have it broken down. For example, here I could describe in unnecessary detail the type of battering ram used. But to get back to the real business at hand; he has brought enormous shame to the family name as a result of his desertion and they have it in their minds to get rid of him. Especially the grandmother – she is the hardest of them all – she would have him crucified for such sinful abandonment of the cross. He had sworn an oath. How glorious it would have been if he had been killed honourably.

From inside the room they can hear the prince ranting gibberish. His voice is raised and with the messy gums and his few remaining teeth all in disorder they can catch only random words, or groans that sound a lot like words. There is no response to their loud entreaties. On the other side of the door, the prince is talking to the severed Saracen head. It's the only thing that truly understands what he's talking about.

With tears streaming down his face, he swears on the Holy Gospels that Crusades are entirely unjust and that there must be no God in heaven at all. It's all a great bloody hoax to claw at money and power. He was informed by fleeing witnesses that in Constantinople it was nothing more than a drunken brawl that set the city on fire – for no good or even discernible reason – the great churches and palaces crumbling and falling into ruins, all the shops and businesses swallowed up by flames of wicked drunken malice; the fleets of burning ships; the bugles sounding, men leaping into the burning ships and with grappling irons pulling them out into the harbour where the main currents would grab them. The noise of the Greeks cheering down by the water's edge as fellow Christians screamed in the dancing flames. Shooting their arrows, hoping to wound or kill as many Franks as they could.

Armed with this news the prince had dug up all his hidden booty, all the pieces of gold and silver, precious stones, lengths of satin and silk, mantles of squirrel fur, ermine and miniver, and every other item wrestled from the hands of the slain. These had been buried outside of their camp. He knew he would need them to get back to Burgundia; to bribe and administer justice; because there was a roaring trade in administering justice to those like him, deserters; and bounty hunters lay waiting in every shady grove along the way back home.

The return journey was just as uneventful as he had hoped. He was cunning enough to pawn off all the armour and even the gauntlets given to him by his grandmother to acquire the status of a destitute beggar; a beggar returning from the war with nothing but a sack containing the severed head of his brother. The prince had aged and browned so well in the unbearable heat that his skin was passably dark and his outfit passably dishevelled to pass him unnoticed. The last of his booty bought him passage on a ship that got him out of that accursed place and back to where the temperatures were now freezing and continuously swept over with mist and rain. How wonderful to be back in this dark and dreary part of the world once more.

While his family members beat down the door of his chambers to go about lynching him, the prince decides that the only rightful course of action is to take his own life. A mortal sin awaits as the Saracen head babbles in its native tongue – offering a gold bezant for every Christian's head; first the prince changes into a fine finishing costume: plain woollen tunic, black-taffeta cape, and hat of white peacock feathers on his neatly combed hair; and then while humming *Veni Creator Spiritus* – opens up his veins with a ceremonial dagger inlaid handsomely with diamond and pearls. In spite of the terrifying din of kettledrums and horns he leaps into the sea, lance in hand, shield hanging from his neck and with helmet tottering, he charges at them, charges in the direction of that mace-wielding horde of dark-skinned heathens, because at this stage there's no point charging in any other direction.

STANDARD OPERATING PROCEDURE

1.0 INTRODUCTION

Somewhere in the region of seven-hundred-and-fifty-thousand medical files are stored in a remote warehouse leased to a well-regarded medical insurance company. The project is as follows: to manually re-organise each file into three distinct sections, digitally scan each section, and upload to the company's state-of-the-art archive and retrieval system. The end result of this endeavour is to ensure that at the push of a button some drone in the Stockholm office or in the Buenos Aires office or in the Dundalk office may easily access a detailed description of Mrs. So-and-So's stool samples. Despite the considerable time and resources invested thus far in the project, acceptable progress has not been achieved.

2.0 SETTING

This warehouse we are speaking of is a cold draughty place – the sound of the same inane radio station echoes through it all day long, as an ongoing crime against sanity. The warehouse is positioned at the end of an otherwise deserted cul-de-sac, in the middle of a derelict industrial estate, two miles from an isolated midlands town. Random graffiti covers gable end brickwork. A shopping trolley containing a traffic cone has been abandoned in the rear car-park. Roads in this estate end abruptly in undeveloped wasteland. All of the other businesses in the industrial estate have failed: their shutters are permanently drawn. Inside this particular warehouse we are speaking about – people feed machines with paper. Talking is not permitted. Break times are strictly monitored. High staff turnover has been identified as a key hindrance to the project's success. The deadline has been extended on four separate occasions. Another extension to the deadline has been sought by the Project Manager. His name is Dunphy; he's currently experiencing a moment of existential crisis in a toilet cubicle.

3.0 REFERENCES

A meeting has been scheduled among the directors in each department of the organisation so they can learn more about the progress of this crucial digitization project. The directors are already seated in a make-shift boardroom; tables have been pushed together and covered with white cloth; there are bottles of still *and* sparkling water. Upside-down glasses stand patiently next to the bottles. At lunchtime a company of caterers will arrive with platters of expensive sandwiches and gourmet coffee. The directors are clock-watching; privately hoping that this bloody thing won't go on too long i.e. all day. They have laptops open – to continue to work on other – more pressing concerns. I have no record of these other concerns.

4.0 RESPONSIBILITY

In the toilet cubicle pale light caresses the forehead of a skeleton. His eyes are hidden within darkened sockets as he witnesses the steady birth and death of droplets. Cramp moves sneakily up the back of both thighs. This is the only place in the whole warehouse where he can hide with immunity. Everything in the digitization project has been building over the last eighteen months – to this moment of truth. He must get the presentation right. If any hope remains of escaping from the warehouse and re-igniting his damp career then this presentation must impress all those assembled. But first he must regain control of bowels that have been vigorously chiming through the morning and the greater part of the previous night.

Inside the boardroom there is a growing sense of unease among the directors. They all want to get started on "this bloody thing" as it has been unlovingly christened. A low hum of mutiny floats in circular fashion around the room and Mr. Sheridan, who checked on Dunphy's whereabouts earlier, is asked what the hell is going on and where is he? Sheridan first colours around the cheeks, before quietly informing the room that Dunphy is still in the toilet. Well perhaps someone should go and check on him? Sheridan already did. Ten minutes ago. Who is the least senior person in the room that can be dispensed to the bathroom to check on Dunphy? With nobody willing to concede seniority Sheridan is sent in there again, muttering angrily.

Moments later, as Dunphy runs through the slides in his presentation, the door of the toilet cubicle is rapped. Dunphy's unwilling to give away his location. The last thing he wants is to identify that it's him with his pants down; fretting, wondering why he *had* to drink that second cup of coffee – half-paralysed (excepting his sphincter) with anxiety, and feeling so very uncomfortable inside his own skin. It would be much better if that person left him alone, to gather his thoughts, to run through them one more time. He silences his breathing by plugging his two lips together. This is supposed to give the impression that he is not there. Where else could he be? The cubicle door is rapped again. Cheeks burning, eyes bulging. He refuses to allow himself be identified. "Dunphy, come on, we're all waiting for you out here," says the owner of the knuckles. "Just be another minute," he hears himself answer, post-exhalation, in a voice that is so wretchedly puny that it only serves to embarrass them both.

When the coast is clear (slammed door) he stands up, trousers bunched around ankles. The sensation of pins and needles is outrageous and connected to the length of time he has been sitting there. It tingles all the way up to his knees. Blood flowing through the capillaries once more. He tries to take a step, and on numbed feet realizes he is stuck fast to the spot where they are planted. Instead he clings to the walls of the cubicle for support. A couple of baby-steps gets him as far as the door. All he can do for the moment is wait; it shouldn't take much longer. Just a few more moments. He checks his watch. A few minutes still to go before he is scheduled to begin. Needless to say he doesn't know that his watch is five minutes slow. What he does know, is that he has a wonderful opening to his presentation. "When you think about it, the mind is a kind of warehouse, isn't it? A warehouse for memories…" He imagines himself saying this line with a confident air, a faintly ironic smirk. "The digitization process we are undertaking is the memory formation in advance of the recall function in this mind…"

Nice opening.

Then let the slides speak for themselves.

It couldn't be easier.

5.0 DEFINITIONS

Stage Fright: the anxiety, fear, or persistent phobia which may be aroused in an individual by the requirement to perform in front of an audience, whether actually or potentially.

6.0 PROCEDURE

It couldn't be any simpler, until he begins to imagine the nitty-gritty, so to speak of the impending presentation; the room an enormous amphitheatre; the sound of voices, of chairs scraping across the floor; briefcases sliding across the table; an odour of sweat from shirt-sleeved armpits; the muttering and sulking and coughing into cupped hands; the audience members scratching themselves around the thighs, adjusting the height of their socks, tapping their pencils on the table, removing eyelashes, sticking pencils in their ears. On the walk from the cubicle to the board-room these images bring with them a trembling nausea that causes him to take a minor detour via the kitchen. He rationalizes the detour by a need for water – his throat feeling dryer than a mouthful of dessert sand on a bed of burnt toast. In the empty kitchen he drinks with a shaky hand that spills water on his shirt, necessitating yet another delay.

Up to this point he had felt in control of his nerves; focused on delivering the key messages contained in his slides. But now the imagined audience grows silent, awaits his introduction; his first slide consists merely of random words without any inter-relationship; in the back of his throat a constriction of the air passage stops him from taking anything but hurried breaths. And though he has prepared meticulously over the previous week, practising what he is going to say, over and over again – at this imagined moment his mind is completely blank. Fantastically blank. And just as his hysteria peaks, a hush, before a sententious voice announces to all present that Dunphy really ought to start over again and stop wasting everyone's time.

Which he does; in a voice so shaky, so unrecognisable – that he is immediately forced to stop. Pretending to consult his notes he takes a series of shallow breaths. After a long silence he tries to begin again, for a third time, but now has developed the hiccups and cannot discern his own hand-writing. His audience writhes in awful silence as he stumbles and falls from word to word. Not one shred of sympathy on any of those expressionless faces. The-hiccup-project-hiccup-by-at-least-hiccup-months. This is the last thing he has to say. Then he curls up like a piece of paper caught in the flame. Voices from all over the room heckle and sneer in loud unctuous voices filled with incredulity. They are of course seeking to impress the Senior Vice President who faces Dunphy at the distant end of the boardroom table. They shake their heads and tut-tut. Frankly from here the fantasy becomes much too ridiculous to describe…

* * *

Dunphy is uncertain that he will be able to get up high enough. The fencing behind the warehouse is easily over eight foot tall. He stands on the shopping trolley and utilizes the peak of the traffic cone, reaches up, grabs hold, pushes off the summit. With an audible grunt he clings on. The fencing rocks with his weight; the only thing he can rely on is his sheer determination to get over the top. His arms strain, his body shudders; in a slug-like manner he glides along the top edge; un-hooks the barbed wire from his pants, closes his eyes, swings down over the other side of the fencing – and plummets through the air, landing on the other side. Turning around he finds himself with a brand new perspective on the derelict wasteland. He wants to run, but will have to make do with limping. He has damaged his ankle ligaments.

Meanwhile Sheridan is being attacked from all sides. No, there is no sign of Dunphy in the toilets. Yes, he did check both cubicles. He doesn't know. He has no idea where Dunphy might be, or could be, but of course he knows where Dunphy should be. Yes, well that has nothing to do with him! A raised venetian blind reveals Dunphy's car is still parked outside. Is this some kind of joke, someone asks? The general consensus is that Dunphy has had another one of his "episodes." Not again. A man without a neck of any description (Director of R&D) slams down his bottle of water. He has better things to do than...sitting here! A search party is organised. Dunphy has to be in the building somewhere. They split up into groups and go looking for the errant executive, calling his name, peering behind the doors, shelving.

7.0 ATTACHMENTS

As Dunphy limps, into the abyss of abandoned buildings and dried-up dog shit – his future life morphs into a single, fast-paced montage: explosions of one realisation after another rock an already damaged internal structure. The explosions are imagined outcomes arising from his decision (taken just now) to permanently escape from the cloying debasement of working in the warehouse. Naturally he could never go back to that place and be jeered at, or even worse, patronised by the same bastards who had taken away all his responsibilities at head office and marooned him in that place. If he would not return to the digitization management role then his position with the well-regarded medical insurance company was untenable. He knew that – they didn't need to tell him that. Naturally the next step would be to tell his ex-wife and handle her myriad questions aimed at him from every angle. This of course would have ramifications in terms of their maintenance agreement, company car, his life assurance, his pension, their health-insurance, his rental property, and the outstanding mortgage payments.

All of these things play on his mind as he turns a corner, an actual corner, and interrupts a scene that has nothing to do with him and in which he ought never to have stumbled upon. Three of them, scrofulous, head-shaven; all wearing remnants from a discarded wardrobe – a bag of clothes dumped onto the floor of a charity shop: mis-matched outfits that do not fit them and seem a long time past current fashions. They are small men or even boys. The three of them regard him with the same mixture of surprise and indignation. This is an alleyway between a dis-used sign factory and a dead garage still oozing oil and grease. The stench of shit is unbearable. Not only are they surprised but they are guilty-faced, for cowering between their knees, he spies an emaciated grey-hound who has been beaten with sticks and yet still whines, pitifully, hopeful that the attack will soon end.

"What you looking at?" snarls one. They are just boys. Another curls his lip to reveal a top row of distended yellow fangs. He takes a threatening step toward Dunphy; carries a pointy stick, the tip stained in blood. "… looks like he's going to cry," exclaims another. The trio double-over with laughter and point their sticks at him. Easy now, easy Alan, don't be a hero, and yet he cannot help but get among them, cannot help swinging fists, slapping ears, pulling hair, gouging eyes; all the while with his own eyes closed, and screaming at the top of his lungs.

8.0 VERSION HISTORY

In an enormous warehouse, belonging to a well-known medical insurance company, housing over seven-hundred-and-fifty-thousand separate medical files, a group of middle-aged men are slipping back on their suit jackets, grimacing awkwardly at each other – while filling their briefcases with the same useless paraphernalia that they dragged along with them to this god-forsaken hell-hole. A convoy of taxis will whisk away these men of industry; back to head office, back to civilization. It really has been a waste of all their mornings. Nevertheless the fact remains that each file in this warehouse needs to be manually re-organised into three distinct sections, digitally scanned and then put up onto the company's system. It says so on the very first of Dunphy's redundant slides. If only the slides really could have spoken for themselves. Instead the overhead projector is powered down and Dunphy is far away, fighting his way through the narrow alleyways – armed with a piece of copper piping, followed by a greyhound who limps, like him, as they try to find a way out of a nightmare of dead-ends, keeping just ahead of the enlarged gang of feral boys who are pursuing them.

WIDOW MAKER

Date of birth: sixteenth of the fourth sixty-one. The doctor's office. My medical file open on his desk. White pages in a grey folder. He's talking to me. I can hear him quite clearly but the words don't go anywhere. They lie wriggling, like dying flies, on his consulting desk, spread over his prescription pad, next to the plastic heart, dotted around his stethoscope. I am sitting right here in front of him. I see his mouth moving. He's bald and wears a paisley tie. He has bad breath. Am I taking it in? No; and it isn't likely to happen anytime soon, either. My wife is with me. She's mopping under her eyes with a bunched up piece of toilet tissue. I was a shambolic mess, naked but for my overcoat, heavily-bearded and discombobulated, when they found me. And now I'm here.

They scare the shit out of you. It's their job. They're trained to do it. You see this – this is what you have. A little diagram on a page of drug-company-sponsored pad. Reduced in the manner they describe it, the very point of living becomes obscure and perfectly ridiculous. The way they condescend and refuse to explain the detail: it's as if we don't want the details or can't be trusted with them; I am a grown man. Just tell me. Don't sugar-coat it. I don't want percentages, recovery-rates, and statistics. Having said all of that I acknowledge the fact that they have a thankless job dealing with people like me: those who refuse to believe that they can die – that the world could possibly continue to exist in their absence. I belong to that school of thought and my belief is unshakeable.

In the darkness I suffocate awake with heavy wheezing lungs. It forces me into a sitting position on the edge of the bed. Accordion lung with catch and whirr of membrane sticking to membrane, mucus clogging the pathways, forcing the air back up your throat and out into the blackness of the room. Reaching deep into the pit of the stomach for a cough that wracks the body. Flinty cough. The bellows strained and old sounding. Priests prayers and Holy medals. All those doctors with their cold stethoscopes and their nodding. Offering no assistance. Gums receded, breath stinking, fingers stained with evidence of nicotine abuse.

Steep stairs lead up to a second-floor office. One at a time. Need take a break. Out of breath. The intervals come more quickly as I climb. Holding tight to the greasy bannister. My breath coming with that same reassuringly dreadful wheeze. The accordion wheeze of diseased lung. The heart still pounding but with uncertainty. As I linger on the stairs I hear tinny music from concealed speakers: transcendental, lilting music. The wallpaper is peeling backwards banana-skin-like from the dampness; the smell of incense disguising the odour of mildew. A voice from above calls down. From the top of the stairs. Do I need some assistance perhaps? Familiar from the phone: the one who took my credit card details.

How had we heard about the healer? Through word-of-mouth. Word-of-mouth had flapped its lips through space and time, had entered war-zones, jumped ravines, spirited through stone walls, to reach my wife. Having no other possible means of correcting my condition we were falling at the feet of a miracle worker. That is correct, a worker of miracles. Just as a matter of interest; how many miracle-workers do you know have a slot free on Tuesday from eleven until twelve in the morning? How many miracle-workers do you know prefer cash? How many miracle workers do you know answer to the name Jude? I'm trying to emphasize how scornful of a positive outcome I was, how much of a waste of time I considered this business to be; and yet, as I struggled up those stairs, my heart hoped as mightily as it hopped: borne out of a sodden desperation.

When I was a child they brought to see a quack. The quack told me to take off my vest. He rubbed ointment over my chest in circles. This went on for a very long time. There were prayers to go along with it too. He told me to say ten Hail Marys and ten Our Fathers before bed. Then he opened his drawer and produced a tiny medal on a length of twine. When he put the medal over my head I can remember an improvement in my breathing. A sense of slight instantaneous relief. It was all in the head. Did I believe in God? Why not? "We're in the temple with Jesus," he kept saying that as he rubbed the stuff into my chest. In bed that night I said the ten of each, as I had been instructed, but the following morning was devastated to discover that my chest was still scalding, still wheezing. I had expected it to be an overnight miracle: I guess we hadn't been in the temple with Jesus after all.

At the top step I pause a few moments. Sweat on my upper lip. Perspiration causing the shirt to stick to my back. I pull aside the young man waiting for me at the top step to ask him what is that instrument playing there? He listens along with me. Above my ancient wheeze. That is the sound of a gamelan, he tells me. A gamelan? As if I should know without further explanation what a gamelan is. But already I am being pointed to a sad little waiting room. Would I like a drink of water? If not then shuffle inside there and sit down quietly. My heart is still racing from the stairs, but certainly no more than a few minutes go by before he returns, wheeling a clunky video cassette player and television on a trolley. With a phenomenally loud whirring noise the video rewinds all the way back to the start. There are other people in the room. I can't bear to make eye-contact with them.

The video should answer all of our questions. In the first part Jude is interviewed by a heavily tanned woman who struggles to read her questions off a page. Either her hand-writing is terrible or this was her first time seeing the questions. The picture quality is poor – grainy, hard to fathom; Jude's face is practically obscured by a withering of the tape. The sound quality is worse. Just as well really: it was insipid stuff. His powers bestowed by the Almighty. All that was required from the visitor was faith. That kind of thing. On it went in the same manner; I could paraphrase it but what difference would that make? All harmless fun – except that I could see the colors splashing over the face of a small child, held on her mother's knee, like a little statue, with hand extended.

Without prior warning the screen split up into rotating amorphous shapes merging and un-merging, swirling by slow moving increments to a medley of trance-like rhythms that grew louder and ever more self-involved. I think it was supposed to put me in a trance; by the end of it I was staring out the window, taking note of how heavy the traffic was, and admiring the ferocity of the rain. This would truly be a miracle because I am not a believer and the video had done nothing to rescue my low expectations. I had been disabused of every notion of faith as a teen when I realized with acute embarrassment that nobody else had ever taken it as seriously as I had; for them it was like getting out of bed in the morning. Not something to consider seriously at all.

Fast-forward through the hour of waiting, a low whirr and the spin of cogs: I'm led toward an office by a faceless and forgettable man. He departs with a polite cough as if saying "I cannot go any further than here." I knock and enter the den of this miracle worker – where I am met by a grimy middle-aged man who looks only vaguely familiar. He's wearing a monogrammed and brazenly expensive shirt topped off with a hideously polka-dotted tie. His hair is running away down the back of his head. Finally I recognize him from the video. God, how poorly he has aged. I start wondering again about that video. My heart sinks lower. You think, it can't get much worse. You're so very wrong. It can always get worse. Much, much worse.

His handshake is brief, cold, and flabby: like squeezing a pack of sausages. I'm instructed to sit down so we can have a little chat about my problem. I take the time to look around; along one wall there's a vast array of dusty old books that have never been opened, a jagged pile of dog-eared pointless magazines, over in the corner a yellow skeleton hangs off a nail driven inexpertly into the wall, on his desk there's a pile of junk-mail and a plastic brain with the different segments colour coded. All of these things are just props; they serve no purpose other than to create the overall effect – but what the effect is supposed to be, completely escapes me.

When I begin to explain my problem to him he doesn't bother to look up. Instead he starts dicking around with his swivel chair. This is a complete waste of time. I'm just another fool in the endless queue, begging for a drop of his precious assistance. I watch him struggle to open the drawer in his desk. When he does manage it, he takes a small yellow card from a big stack held together by a rubber band. He starts asking me questions: How old am I? Where do I work? Am I married? Children? Why not? Since when? He doesn't look at me, not once, not one time during the whole rigmarole. He's simply going through the motions. He could be working behind a cash register in a fast-food restaurant; as a waitress in a cocktail bar; he could be amputating my legs. Then he tells me to lie-back on the couch.

He comes over, places a pair of heavy over-sized head-phones over my ears, goes back to his desk the other side of the room, and starts speaking softly into a microphone. Can I hear him clearly? Yes, I can hear him. I give him the thumbs up. He instructs me in no more than a whisper to lie back and relax, to listen to the sound of his voice, to enter a state of light trance, just the slightest state of light trance, just to relax and gently breathe in-and-out, in-and-out. That's it. My eyelids are getting heavier and heavier; then lighter, fluttering like butterflies; then heavier – resting, resting, resting. It is a very relaxing experience, if nothing else. Just lying there, listening to the sound of his voice. He begins to describe a scenario:

"Imagine you are walking through a beautiful field; see how wonderfully green is the grass all around you. Breathe-in that scent of freshly cut grass. Smells good, doesn't it? Now you follow a river; the sound of the babbling water lapping against the stones brings you even further into a state of perfect relaxation. I want you to take a deep breath and really savor the lovely clean air. Think how lovely and pink your lungs are and how healthy they feel. Aahh! Now, that's good isn't it? Of course there is a forest nearby here, a pine forest that you skirt around in a completely relaxed frame of mind. Smell those pine cones…uhmm! See that boy standing there by the gate. Yes, that one. Go to him and take him by the hand. Yes, he is a trusting little fellow. Now both of you walk towards the forest."

Jude takes a break to hack up some phlegm then continues: "Imagine there is a house in the forest. Yes, that's right a little cottage in a clearing. No need to knock, just enter with the boy. See the woman standing by the window. She's fretting because her son was lost – but look, you have just returned him. A warm smile spreads over her soft pink face as the boy runs to her and is lifted gently up to her heaving firm bosom. Feels good doesn't it? Everything is going to be alright from now on; everybody is safe and sound; there is absolutely no possibility of that boy going missing again because you are going to stay here and be watchful, you are going to make sure it never happens again, never, never, never…"

Then, before I know it, I am sitting up, wiping the tears away with thankful shame, and handing him back the headphones. He presents me with an inexpertly laminated piece of cardboard that says – *Never, Never, Never* along with a tape cassette recording of our session. I do not bother to tell him that I do not possess a cassette player, like the vast majority of people belonging to the first world. Is that it? Over already? He nods and sits back in his chair so as to give himself a triple-chin. Yes, we are all done and I may now leave his presence. He instructs me to pay on the way out, if I have not already done so, and turns his attention to a fleck of dirt on his shirt.

* * *

Let me rewind the tape to my most recent attack which took place in our back-garden. I'm bent over, unable to clear my lungs, heart thumping wildly. My nephew continues to play on. He thinks I'm play-acting. His suspicion is that if he comes over to see what's wrong I'll steal the ball and score on him. To be fair: it's like something I would do. In the background I hear him celebrating. I cannot speak or breathe. My wife sees me from the window. My head turning to a beetroot color. In the ambulance they put a mask over my nose and mouth. All the melodrama reduced to a single breath, just one single puncture of breath slowly leaking into my lungs. It can happen any time. At night I reach out for my wife; she turns on the light, slaps me on the back; gets herself worked up into hysterics. She's frightened; at her wits end. Other people can do it. Why not me? What makes me so different to everyone else?

It has to stop but it won't. Tonight I sit out the back of my local bar; I'm hidden behind a rusty old barbecue and a stack of disused patio chairs. It's the middle of summer; the sun is genuinely shining. Moments ago I begged one from an acquaintance. Didn't even have to ask. My pleading expression said it all. The lid of the box flips back and I have it right here, stuck between yellowed fingers. Put it into the ashtray and wedge it firmly down in the notch. Sit back and watch it burn with the strip of flame slowly turning the paper and tobacco to greyish ash. How could any of this exist without me, to witness it? Now if you'll excuse me – I have this cigarette to smoke and my drink to drink.

THE ACCURSED

Dear Janet & Mark,

You won't remember me but I was at your recent wedding. You won't remember me because I didn't introduce myself outside the church like everyone else. There was a moment when I was going to, but then someone's aunt interrupted, to point at the clouds – suggesting you get a move on – the forecast was bad. I used that opportunity to slip-past, because frankly – when you don't know either bride or groom it's a little bit awkward, that moment, I find. I was the plus-one of Janet's third cousin, Lulu. The reason I'm writing is that since your "big day" my life has gone down the toilet and I think it may have something to do with events at the wedding itself. I know it sounds completely ludicrous but I honestly do believe that I was cursed that night, or else brought a nasty enchantment on myself, by being too stingy to buy a round of drinks.

You seem like such a nice couple. Here, let me congratulate you both on making such a wonderful decision. Kiss on both cheeks for you Janet. Firm hand-shake for Mark. She really is a beauty and not nearly as anorexic-looking as the people at my table kept insinuating during the meal. And he's not so bad either Janet, is he – since the dental work? It couldn't have happened to two nicer people. And I'm not just saying that – I really do mean it. The speeches by the way were excellent.

Especially the father of the bride. Most of the time it doesn't work when you read the whole thing off a piece of paper held in a shaky hand; but in this instance it worked out just fine. His touching story about your grandfather decapitating a prisoner of war, especially went down well, from where I was sitting.

I'm the guy who refused to buy a round of shots. I'm the one who accepted a slurred invitation to join a round and then welched on the deal. It all started when a guy pointed to my glass and made a motion with his hand. I should have said no. I realize that now. Instead I acquiesced. A dip of eyebrow and a slight nod. It was stupid of me. I just wish I could apologize to that group individually – I think there were seven; the un-surity on my part stems from being slightly tipsy at the time and losing count of the shot glasses on the tray. I know what you're thinking – the tight git – serves him right! But please, please hear me out. The punishment does not fit the crime.

Yes; I admit it – I swallowed that drink like the other six souls in the round; since then everything, every damn thing has gone wrong for me. Absolutely every single thing; originating with the thought that scorched my mind as the alcohol scorched the back of my throat, bringing bile up from my stomach: namely – *"I'm not buying a round for these people."* The rationalization came running to catch up: *"I don't know any of them."* So, having swallowed the shot and screamed with the others, tie pulled up around my forehead, I ducked out of the reception room and made a break for the toilets.

On my way there I passed a couple who were arguing. She held his face in her hands and I heard her say: "take it easy, please, on the drink, for me…" Such a big red face he had. Already stocious drunk. The next time I would see him that night he was fist-pumping anyone who would make eye contact, for no reason whatsoever; which is why there was a two metre radius exclusion zone around him early in the night – until we had all clambered up to his plateau of insanity.

I did my business and waited in the cubicle for a few minutes. To cool down; everyone was in agreement that the reception room was broiling. As I'm blowing cold air on myself there is a commotion: shouting, doors slamming. "She wasn't even pregnant!" screams the voice. That same somebody was banging on the closed cubicle doors, working his way down along them. Each open door clunked against the wall as he kicked it inwards with an accompanying dull wooden echo. Such was my sense of guilt I assumed he was looking for me, to buy the others a drink. He banged and kicked the door of my cubicle but he was so drunk that I couldn't understand what he was saying, something about it all being a terrible mistake…too late now…

I couldn't say how long I was in there before the idiot left. Could have been five or ten minutes but when I emerged like a secretive creature, so careful and timid, all I wanted to do was wash my hands and get the hell out of there. No hand-soap, by the way. Not that you should have been checking the bathroom regularly, but just thought I'd mention it, for again. So I made do with a breath-mint from the basket. The mint made up for the hand-soap. But it was immediately knocked out of my mouth when I stepped outside the toilets by a small stump-like creature roaring at me to take the viscous red liquid from her and to "get it down me." Despite the ooze between my fingers I downed most of it with only a small bit spilling on my jacket sleeve.

Had she been waiting outside the toilet all that time? I don't know. I guess that she had because as soon as I downed the disgusting stuff, having watched me do it with her big watery red eyes twitching, her mouth curled into a disdainful furl – she ripped the shot glass out of my hand and walked away without another word in my direction. That should have been my cue to run and order a round of drinks, for my new friends. Instead I slunk through the bar with my head bowed and went searching for Lulu. We had become separated earlier in the night when she wanted to dance; I don't like to boogie. Fine for other people but not me. No, I won't do it. She tried to drag me out on the dance-floor but I dug in my heels and almost took the table with me as she grabbed my jacket sleeve and tugged with all of her might. And when somebody's cousin tapped her on the shoulder I was relieved of my duties and returned to the drinks on the table with my usual gusto.

It was only when the music took that particular turn for the worst that I knew I would have to get out of there – but it was already too late – the conga line had formed and it swallowed me whole as my hands met the gyrating hips of a game grunting grandmother, my own pinioned by an over-enthusiastic reveller whose bosoms kept a jumping from her dress. I don't know if you were part of the conga line, but if you were not, then let me describe the horror of it to you. Not content with snaking around the tables and dance floor it decided to go out a side-door, past a huddle of smokers and into the almost complete darkness of the surrounding gardens. It was not funny. It was not amusing. I tried to break free but the human chain entangled me as soon as I did and I was thrust back into my place again with stern words from outraged revellers.

Finally it found its way back in through a fire-exit and we were released from the chain. But even then I could not escape because that same fist-pumping psychotically drunk man I mentioned earlier grabbed me like a front-row forward entering a scrum and demanded that I, in turn, grab someone else. We had to form a circle. It took a long time to locate you both. When you were admitted to the centre of the circle I was dragged inwards and outwards in nauseating waves of pointless-ness. You both did so well to feign enjoyment although I will say that the masks did seem to slip when we attempted to chair-lift you both and go searching for a non-existent garter up those long legs of the terrifically blushing bride. It went too far and once again I apologize but want to make it abundantly clear that I was just following orders; it was the red-faced man made me do it.

When I saw the opportunity open up for me I quite literally ran for the exit. Even now it feels dream-like. Running through a wall of cus-tard. Arms and legs pumping. Sweat on brow pouring. Fighting my way through the gauntlet of restraining arms and legs. Sending people flying in every direction. Not listening to the cries and yelps of those unlucky enough to stand or dance in my way. Until a voice that I recognised hauled me back to the reality of what I was doing. Lulu was shouting in my face. She wanted me to sit down with her because she had something she needed to ask me. We sat down at a random table amongst strangers. "Are you depressed?" she screamed, loudly, on account of the loud music. She seemed convinced that I was depressed and not only that but it was bringing her down too. Obviously she was drunk. I assured her that I was not depressed and reminded her that I did not like weddings, remember?

"Are you sure?" she insisted, "Because you seem like someone who is depressed?" Again I did my best to impress upon her my dislike for weddings; that this was only a temporary impediment to our shared happiness, but she seemed far more interested in the activities of a man at the bar. He was openly staring at her. His tongue was hanging out. His hair matted to his head with sweat. It was the one who had been dancing with her while I was off in the conga, doing my duty. Lulu decided that it would be best if we switched to being just friends, from that exact moment, going forward. I didn't want her to see how upset I was so I nodded, and nodded some more as she explained unnecessarily her lack of romantic feelings for me and all the while kept catching his eye at the bar.

"You can stay on, if you want, it's up to you," she said and gave me a sexless peck on the cheek. With that she stood up, walked over to the man at the bar, and attached herself by the mouth so that they became like a pair of leeches; sucking, twirling, fondling, groping, sliding along the bar; falling over a table; rolling around the floor and finally disappearing behind a couch; after which they were never seen again. At this point someone tried to pull a Christmas cracker with me but I refused to tug on it. Instead I went outside and sat alone beneath those parasols you had arranged in the moonlight. Maybe I was depressed. Maybe I ought to have left everyone else enjoy themselves without my leering unhappiness impinging.

Then I felt something crawling around my hair. I looked up

and between the parasols there was a single piece of rope along which a single file "conga-line" of ants was moving. But at least they were doing something productive because on their backs they carried pieces of leaves, twigs, other little items for purposes unknown – and some were falling off the edge of the rope because it was not single-file but a melee of over and back. Although I moved out of the way there was no escaping the fact that I had ants crawling on my head and some had even taken a trip down the back of my shirt. So I spent some considerable time shaking myself off and swearing. There may even have been tears. I can't say for certain, but I do know that by the time I had finished there was another shot sitting on a tray, by the chair where my jacket was hanging. I didn't see who had left it for me.

Well after the bad news from Lulu and the ants and the general misery (by now I was depressed) the shot was delivered straight down the gullet with a minimum of fuss. It tasted like cough medicine and was a disgusting green colour. Then the father of the bride decided to give me a lecture. Quite the character isn't he? I mean the speech was bad enough, but to follow it up with a personal lecture was too much, even for me. Again I can only apologize for my behaviour and wish that the circumstances leading to his broken ankle were different; but honestly – it was such a gentle push, and I had no idea there was a step right behind him. And to be fair I *did* help him back to his seat – which is where I insulted Mark's sister.

I genuinely did think she was lesbian. Don't ask me why, but I promise that I got that vibe off her. It was because while trying to explain to her why this country is going down the drain; she kept frowning and when she said something about her partner I thought she was referring to a woman sitting next to her at the table. You see how it was all starting to unravel for me! It wasn't my fault. I did try to be nice and chatty but your father was groaning in agony and there was an ambulance on the way. Then another shot arrived. Once again I didn't see who had left it in front of me. Naturally I drank it quick as a flash – feeling my pulse rise – and a vein in the side of my head begin to throb.

After that things are hazy and muddled. I distinctly remember a group of women crying outside. They could have been bridesmaids come to think of it. They were trying to take an umbrella away from some crazed lunatic with mascara all over her face who was smashing glasses off tables. I did try but she wouldn't allow me to help her. She was in a state. "Follow her – this could be the best night of your life," someone said.

Next image: a whirling room of lights and over-loud chart music. I was offered cake. It must have been the wedding cake. I didn't get a big enough piece so I tried to help myself, which is when the accident happened. Again all I can do is apologize profusely for the collapse of the second tier. But I do believe that there must have been something wrong with the base layer, the foundations if you like, because all I did was push the knife in (while partaking of another shot), and then…

I'm rambling again and perhaps by this stage you're thinking "So fucking what!" or else "Who is this loser?" but I want to impress upon you the fact that nothing particularly bad had ever happened to me throughout my entire life, until the night of your wedding. Nothing particularly great either but that's not the point. The point is – what did I do to deserve this? That's the question I've been plaguing myself with these last couple of weeks. I've been a good boy, I've always done exactly what was expected of me – so why, as a direct result of attending your wedding did I lose my long-term girlfriend, crash my car the following morning into a stationary wall, lose my driving licence after a positive breathalyser, and then my lucrative sales position with a highly reputable pharmaceutical company? Why did all these awful things happen as a consequence of what should have been a wonderfully happy occasion?

By wracking my brain the only reasonable explanation I can come up with is that by reneging on the deal, by ducking out of the round of drinks, by deciding in my bitter and twisted mind-set that I would never see any of these people again so what difference did it make: by making this selfish decision I managed to bring an almighty curse on my own head. I appreciate how tiresome it would be at this stage to get a complete list of names to allow me to contact each potential member of that round, but I believe that as the married couple around whom the whole day revolved – that if you could find it in your hearts to absolve me – then and only then – do I believe my life can get back on track.

Until I hear a response from you I will continue to eat pre-packaged meals and shuffle around my apartment like the most pathetic edifice of man you could possibly drag yourself to imagine. I'm begging you. Please lift the curse by whatever means you see fit. Perhaps just by reading this letter it will lift. Until then I wait in fear for the coming of another doom-laden day and night. Please, please, please; help this broken man repair what's left of a sad and pathetic existence. Do what you can to help me. For your pity, your charity, your good-naturedness – I will be eternally grateful, etc., etc.

Yours Sincerely

(Signature illegible)

P.S. So glad you didn't go through with the annulment.

INTERVIEW WITH A CAMPFIRE

W hat the newspaper did next set the tone for the whole day. Sporting tight brown trousers and dainty black shoes, it emitted a sound akin to upholstery being ripped apart. There was a very faint quiver of the front page but no apology – not even an acknowledgement of the fact. While I muttered with indignation a sulpher-like stench slowly engulfed the train carriage. Incidentally, the photograph on the front page was still of a dog shaking hands with a politician. It was standing up tall on its hind legs (the dog) and looking disdainfully at the future leader of this country. It was a very unusual dog – a cross between a Labrador and a Poodle. There were names underneath. Of course I was more interested in the dog's name but the writing was too small to make it out.

For the remainder of the journey I was troubled by a complete lack of enthusiasm for the interview I was travelling towards. To be quite honest I considered it beneath me; but rather than stay on the train and wait for it to go back the way we came, I got off at the small deserted station and walked into the nearby town. The morning sun cast a disconcerting orange light across cars and trees and buildings. Walking past the window of a men's outfitters I noticed a mannequin in the window. I stopped in my tracks and stared. It reminded me vaguely, of someone. It had the likeness of a young man with short black hair and a piercing gaze. His head tilted at an unusual angle – it may have been incorrectly screwed on – and his hands were frozen in karate-chop positions. Despite my very best efforts I could not for the life of me figure out who it reminded me of.

Upon my arrival at the factory I found the entrance to be unmanned. There were clearly people working inside the bowels of the factory – the car park was full, but there was nobody at the security hut and no sign of activity behind the tall security gates. I thought I could hear, coming from the factory buildings, a dull repetitive thudding noise off in the distance, a terrible odious monotonous thud, thud, thud, of some heavy object pounding against a blackened earth, but when I stopped to deliberately listen for it – the thudding went away, and it was only when I stopped listening for it, that it started again.

My eyes scanned the security gate for some sign of entry: a red button, sticking out like an erect nipple required pressing – so I pressed it. From the intercom box a woman's plaintive voice answered, told me to wait for the buzz and then push the gate. I waited for the buzz. Nothing happened. I had no option but to press the red nipple again. She came over the intercom once more. She repeated the same instructions; wait for the buzz and then push. I did not push until I heard the buzz and when I heard the buzz (or what I thought must be the buzz) I pushed but the thing still wouldn't move. So I had to press the nipple again. The woman was so angry that she went silent and so I babbled about my predicament. Eventually she came out of a building, walked swiftly towards me, and pulled the gate open with the greatest of ease.

Without so much as a glance in my general direction she turned on her heels and walked away smartly, her large behind swerving quite dramatically from side to side, back towards a squat red brick building at the end of a series of grey concrete paving slabs. I was admitted to an empty waiting room furnished with a row of drab plastic chairs along the walls and a low coffee table in the middle, smothered in old dog-eared magazines. My eye roved from one barren wall to the next. It was a depressing kind of a place.

After a long time sitting there I'm nearly asleep, when out of nowhere another small plump woman in a smart suit appears in the doorway with a clip-board clenched to her bosom. I am perkily instructed to follow her. We walk up two flights of stairs and down a long dimly lit corridor at the end of which I am asked to wait in a small room consisting of just a single chair and an empty water dispenser. According to *this* woman – they are nearly ready for me.

The clock high on the wall across from me says eight forty-nine. I watch time go past with the jerky, continuous movement of a red plastic hand as it stops – then carries on – past each tiny gradation. After precisely six minutes and thirty-eight seconds I stop watching the clock but when I close my eyes I can still picture that red hand jerking along in a steady monotonous onslaught. Eventually she comes back and leads me into a boardroom, a long narrow room with a long narrow table down the center and a number of chairs pushed in neatly all along it. It is a really nice table – dark wood, expertly polished, smooth to the touch: I really can't say enough good things about the table, it's even the perfect height for resting my elbows on.

I hear the sound of footsteps coming down the hallway and then the door of the room opens. I rise from my chair to exchange handshakes with an HR woman who looks very like an ostrich: long neck, black beady-eyes, short cropped haircut, and with a puffball body encased in a power suit. Right alongside her is the site Technical Director – a lumbering dead-ringer for an albino gorilla; thick-set and in a terrifically grumpy mood. The ostrich does the introductions and starts waffling on about the company: established in blah-blah-blah; over two hundred something or others; chief exports, who gives a damn. There's a large window in the space between their heads and I gaze out through it. Beyond the walls of the factory there are fields made green by that still strong morning sunlight, I see clouds hued pink in an azure sky, I can also see a distant figure walking its dog and throwing a stick-like object for the dog to retrieve, quite possibly a stick.

Ostrich

So tell us a little bit about yourself?

It depends on who you ask. If you were to ask my ex-wife I'm a demon of some sort; a cruel and sadistic schemer who doesn't give a damn about his children. She accuses me of walking away from my responsibilities and not giving her the credit she feels entitled to – for the great job she's done raising the kids. If you ask my friends they will tell you that I am unreliable and only contact them when I'm broke and looking for a hand-out. But my friends and family don't really know me at all. That's the thing. I like to keep myself hidden from view. I want to share a secret with you – I am actually the reincarnation of St. Stephen (Died A.D. 34, Jerusalem). I know it's incredible but what do you want me to tell you – a bunch of make-believe lies about my previous experience in the frozen meat industry? I only discovered my true identity last month through a series of visions I experienced during hot yoga class.

The Ostrich is extremely happy with the answer I've provided. She's so delighted she grimaces with a smile and writes a few highly ornate notes in the margins of my CV. She has a bit of something stuck to her upper lip. Perhaps it is cream from a cappuccino or else some kind of ointment for a cold sore? What is she writing down, I wonder? And why hasn't she made reference to, or even glanced at my tonsure yet? The albino gorilla takes off his designer glasses and deftly wipes them with a little cloth he has conjured from somewhere, most likely from his anal passage. It's a little yellow cloth imprinted with the name and address of his local optician. When they are scrupulously clean of smudges, dry-skin, eyelashes, he slides them back on in a remarkably gentle fashion and puts the little cloth back where it belongs. He glances down at his belly and removes a few bits of fluff from his rather conservative green tie.

Gorilla

Why did you leave your last job?

Because they did not want to hear the truth – that's why. They shouted and covered their ears, they rushed at me and they sentenced me to be stoned to death. I brought up the whole "he who hath not sinned bit" and the stones started flying (they must have brought them into work in their briefcases), so I hid under the board room table and used the Managing Director (Tom-something) as a human shield to get the hell out of there. But you know something, it's like I always say – "was there ever a prophet that they didn't try and persecute?" You know what I mean? I'm just going to take a drink of water here at this juncture, I've gone fierce thirsty all of a sudden

The gorilla nods his head in understanding. I'm giving him another one of those textbook answers. They are a basic requirement – any hint of individual thought is exterminated by stock answers to stock questions; the round ball goes in the round hole; 2 and 2 equals four; that's all the examples I can think of right now. He produces a banana and peels it gently as I continue to wax lyrical about the benefits of gaining experience in a multitude of different settings, which is short-hand for being run out of every job I've ever had because of my lack of interest in working. As he lovingly devours the banana his ostrich colleague buries her head in the sands of ignorance. If she would only just open her eyes and look at me: my tie not tightened, top shirt button undone, mis-shaven faced, pink-eyed from the previous night, and worst of all I'm not even wearing shoes with the suit – I'm sporting trainers with the insignia blackened by a permanent marker.

Ostrich

What motivates you to do a good job?

Money motivates me. I can't think of any other reason for wanting to work in a meat processing plant. I mean if I was to try and explain it to one of my children, if I was to say "Daddy is going into work to further process cuts of meat into cheaper portions to go into dog food and slightly better cuts for the Eastern European market" would that kid's eyes light up? I don't think they would. Not unlike every other person who gets up in the morning when they don't want to, travels into work at a job they dislike and stays working all day with this great pretense that it's really not that bad once you get into it – I work to pay off my debts. Some people buy into the whole business and enjoy repeating the company slogans and admonishing those who ignore them and I understand and respect that: if you want to convince someone of a lie then you better believe it yourself, I get that - but I'm here for the hard cash Ms. Ostrich. Next question please.

Gorilla

What are your strengths and what are your weaknesses?

My strength, Mr. Gorilla, is that I can't stand other people. I hate the fucking sight of them. I hate people and I hate work and I hate clocking-in and clocking-out and pretending. More than anything I hate pretending to be interested in the field of work I find myself wandering around in. So you see by not giving a shit it actually helps because it gives me the cold dispassionate eye one needs to survive in this kind of environment. And I can tell an asshole when I see one which is what you clearly are. I can well imagine taking orders from you and never doing things up to your expected standard. How long would it take for us to fall out I wonder? A month, two months...who knows. My weaknesses are literally too numerous to mention but I'll have a go; I'm lazy, I don't listen, I hate taking orders, I am un-sociable and prone to bullying people when they bug me...that's all I can think of right now.

Ostrich

Stephen why should we hire you?

For a brief moment I am inexplicably thrown by the question. My mouth opens and then closes without a word passing my lips. I stare into those two sets of expectant eyes and I do not know what to say. Nothing! There is not one word in my mind that presents itself for usage. They are shying away from the act of bravery. They seek safety in the silence of the crowd. Instead there is an excruciating stillness in the room where the ticking of the wall clock becomes deafening. I'm like that mannequin.

I'm like that dummy in the shop window, hands frozen in karate chops, eyes glazed over, head screwed on at a bizarre angle; I'm staring at the world through thick glass and all I see are people walking past me and the ones who do turn their heads see nothing more than a young mannequin in trousers and matching jumper, they don't see the real me – the first martyr of Christianity – they see an eye-catching ensemble put together by some window-dresser with rough hands. Then I hear myself vomit out the following:

I believe that I have the relevant experience to do the job. I believe that I've proved myself more than capable in the past. I believe I would be an excellent addition to the team here at this well-regarded company. I am excited at the prospect of learning more and growing both as an individual and as a team player within this exciting organization and who knows? I think I would make a really significant contribution to the company and bring renewed success through my hard work and results-based dynamism.

The Ostrich nods her head emphatically and locks eyes with the Gorilla who shrugs his shoulders as much as to say "I've no more interest in this than a colonoscopy." The Ostrich thanks me for coming in to see them and she keeps smiling at me now. Well done, for answering all the questions in a way that has meant we can tick all the boxes. Well done for making our lives that little bit easier. Well done for telling us nothing that we need be concerned about. Well done. Is there anything I'd like to ask them?

I'm gazing out through that large window between their heads. Beyond the high grey walls of the factory there are luscious bountiful meadows made green by the holiest of morning light. The heavens are opening, I can see a distant figure being mauled by a dog. I jump to my feet and send the chair toppling over. It has all gone too well, this interview – I need to create a diversion to get out of here – like a distant figure being mauled by a dog.

"Christ Almighty look what's happening out there!" I shout. The intention is that they turn their heads and I'll bolt from the room, but when the time comes, my two hands are clamped to those of the gorilla, in a vice-like handshake; he wants to know how soon can I start? And also to apologize for that business earlier in the train carriage.

TINKERMAN

Not all roads in this locality are named. Maps don't explain areas known only by allusions to obscure not-so-recent events. You need to be from round here to fully understand what I'm saying. The place I'm talking about is set right on the tip of a vast icy lake. Stunning views. Just absolutely stunning; and I'm not just saying that because of my occupation. Really, the view is outstanding. A very discrete entrance to the property: recessed cattle-grid; simple iron gate; an extended winding causeway between interlaced black trees; darkness always – on account of the trees; and enormous glacial boulders standing guard in a rough circular pattern.

Being outsiders they had to follow me in their car.

It was the view of the lake that had attracted them. Or so they kept insisting. She especially, in that querulous whisper. The view, yes but more than that, the isolation was what they really wanted: to be left alone. Their privacy being excessive, fanatical, even then. To get so much as a sliver of information out of them was torturous. For me it's important to know a certain amount about people before leasing them a property; it's common sense. I don't want hassle with a tenant. Especially with them being outsiders. He claimed to be a teacher; and she...something about performance art. Whatever that means. All a little vague, even then – but I couldn't help but be attracted to them. Despite their odd and secretive natures.

It was quite obvious on the day that they viewed the property that they did not tolerate others. Despite pretending to be oblivious I was struck by just how agitated they were by my presence, in what they had already decided was their new lair. When they moved into the property a week later, they were horrified by my insistence on going through every item of the lease in painstaking detail. Perhaps I enjoyed it, seeing them squirm with impatience, even going so far as to pretend that my pen was not working. Yes, perhaps I enjoyed that moment of panic in their eyes as I shook it and joked - that maybe it was a sign. And when their signatures were drying on the paper – how they longed to escape my inane questions. Despite their reluctance I forced them to take my business card and to promise to contact me if they needed anything – we were a vibrant community – there was always something going on in the village: amateur dramatics, the farmers market, cinema nights – there was no reason why they shouldn't join in the fun.

That was in late August. I'm sure the exact date is written down somewhere. From that date onwards, in fact from the moment I handed them the keys, nobody in the community set eyes on them. I know because I made numerous subtle inquiries from time to time in the local shop, the pub, the petrol station – over the course of the weeks and months that followed. Nobody had seen them. Nobody even knew they were living there. When I described what they looked like to local people, they shook their heads, had no clue who I was talking about.

Coming up to Christmas it occurred to me to go and pay them a friendly visit. The weather was particularly atrocious on that occasion; it was so bitterly cold by the lake with a wind whipping and shearing through my coat that as I tried to access the site with a gift-wrapped bottle of whiskey under my armpit, I was half-tempted to postpone it to another time. But I was curious. There's no point denying it. However at the entrance causeway to the site I discovered a fallen tree so mangled into place behind the cattle grid that it completely barred access. From the car I tried to call the phone number I had been given. No answer. To do something about the fallen tree meant contacting the owner, and being Christmas, it took a few days for him to get back to me.

In the meantime I had made several more attempts to contact them. There was a thick forest either side of the causeway that contained deep crevasses hidden by a matted strangulation of wild vegetation. I wasn't willing to take that chance. Otherwise I could get there via boat; which seemed excessive. Instead I waited a few days and accompanied the tree surgeon. In no time at all he had carved a way for me to squeeze through with his ear-splittingly loud chainsaw. From the cattle-grid to the house was another couple of minutes by foot in darkness. Naturally I was alarmed: If I couldn't get in – then how had they managed to get out? And there was the question of who was liable if something had happened, God forbid!

The car they had followed me to the property with was parked up against one of the huge glacial standing rocks at what appeared to me as a strange angle. The closer I came the more wrong it looked, until I was close enough to see that it was stuck there head first: the front of the car was crushed, the lights broken, the hood bent out of shape so that it looked as if the car had been driven at speed and repeatedly into the rock to cause so much damage.

With my sense of alarm now spilling over into an uncomfortable dread, I looked to the nearest window in the house. The woman was standing there, stock-still, staring out at me, expressionless. "He's here!" she screamed "Tinkerman is here." Then she moved away from the window, disappearing into the un-seen interior of the house. Despite knocking on the back door and on the windows neither she nor the man would come out or answer my requests. I realized that I'd made a very serious error of judgement in allowing them to have the property. There was clearly something very wrong with them.

Once the tree surgeon had carved up the fallen tree into manageable chunks, I helped him heap them into the back of his trailer. "Everything ok?" he asked. It must have been showing on my face as I slammed those heavy pieces of sawed-up trunk into the metal flooring. I told him everything was just fine – when in fact I was furious, furious with myself, for allowing these outsiders to come in and take over a property that they had no claim on, furious for not following up on their references at the time, furious for allowing my gut feeling to be upstaged by admiration. It was entirely my fault. Now I would have to notify the owner (a kindly old man with no stomach for confrontation), contact the local authorities, initiate court proceedings and fuck-knows what else to get them out.

That night I returned home and once inside the door tore away the gaudy Christmas wrapping from around the bottle of whiskey, and with a sudden twist, snapped the neck. A hot feeling down the back of my throat and then a burning sensation in my chest. I collapsed in front of the television and stared into that empty rectangle where my reflection was ready to drink itself into oblivion. What could her description "Tinkerman" possibly mean? They must have talked about me in such a tone that I was afforded a nick-name to distinguish me from others. What did they say about me? There was a chance, wasn't there? There was a chance that she was being kept there against her will. A narrative began to slowly unfurl with each sip of whiskey: an unlikely hero's journey.

In the small print of every lease, I have always insisted on the right to inspect a property at a mutually agreeable time and date. Having made three calls to the tenants to arrange these details, with no response from their side – I took it upon myself to choose a day and a time that suited me. Armed with a spare key I arrived at the property, pulled up alongside the ditch, and saw that they had barricaded the entrance causeway once again – for make no mistake about it – they had forced the tree down the first time around. In this instance they had used smaller rocks and branches torn off the trees to construct their barrier.

All of this was illegal. Completely against all local laws. It made me angry to think of them giving two-fingers to me, and to the local community by barricading themselves inside a property and ignoring people who only wanted to be friendly towards them. Perhaps their rejection of my friendship was what stung most. It outraged me to think they could just come here, take over, and tell us to keep out. The bloody cheek of them. If they wanted to live here – they should abide by our rules. They should integrate into our local community. Be respectful to the way we live our lives. Did they really think this stupid cairn would keep us out?

I smashed my way through it in a fury; I kicked the smaller stones aside, rolled the heavier ones down into the deep ditches, pulled at the branches until I had a clear path, then got back into my jeep and sped down the causeway. By now I was sweating and red-faced with anger. I drove across the cattle-grid and it produced a loud clattering clang of warning for the couple. I drove through the dark corridor of trees with my full headlights on, not knowing what to expect next.

Parking next to their car wreck I looked up to the same window as before but she was not there. I walked around the back of the property. I did the decent thing and knocked repeatedly on the door. With nobody willing to answer, I used my key and turned the lock.

Inside the property was far worse than I could have possibly imagined. They had torn out every piece of furniture in the entrance hallway and kitchen. Every table, every chair, the dresser, all the cabinets, all the carpets torn-up, everything with respect to furnishings and fixtures had been pulled from the walls and floors. I tried the light switch, nothing. The hanging fixtures pulled clean out of the plasterboard. No lights working anywhere, not in the hallway, kitchen, living room. They had gutted the place like a fish – pulled the bones out – leaving only the fleshy walls. Bare walls. All wallpaper had been stripped clean off. Floorboards in the master bedroom pulled up to expose the grey concrete beneath them. All the while I was shouting for them as I inspected the carnage, shouting for them to come out of wherever they were hiding.

I took out my phone to call the nearest Garda station. To my mind this was a crime scene. But there was no coverage. No way to contact anyone by phone. And now the hangover and my shaking hands, I was frightened, unsure what to do, leave or investigate further? Then I heard the moaning. A continuous long low moan. My hand tightened around the weapon in my pocket: a small claw hammer, as I followed the sound. It was so hard to locate the source, a muffled sound, only faintly audible. Was it coming from outside?

There's a small shed. A boat-house. Closer to the water's edge. Go then. Down to the boat-house. As if being drawn there in a dream trance. The moaning louder. Louder muted moaning. Open the boat-house door. The emaciated naked figure trapped in a rough cage. A wooden cage. The eyes downcast. Moaning like a beast. The woman naked but not caged. Full-breasted, lacquer-eyed, hungry. She speaks to the creature in the cage "See I told you he would come! I told you the Tinkerman would come for me." She points to the cage and nods her head. It must be done quickly and without any more of this undue suffering.

Outside the boat-house a full moon. My head swirls from the crisp air. Torrents of white moonlight shred the darkness. Enormous un-rolled ferns forming a creeping guard of honor along the overgrown cinder path as I drag him along. The wind blows his lank black hair back into his open eyes. Following her flaming torch, we struggle down the slip-ramp to where the boat waits, still bobbing on the lap of waves. Careful in the manner of handling the body. We place him at the prow, resting his back against the smoking pyre. We push the craft out into the moon's dappled reflection and watch the sparks jump and dance into the darkness.

But all of that happened such a long time ago. Before our marriage: celebrated in the orange glow of the funeral fire; a hurried formality before the barricade was rebuilt and my jeep put beyond use. Before the cage that I would require had been hastily constructed from the remnants of the floor-boards. Before the strength to fight-back or even argue left my slender body for good. Now safe in my cage, the dull screams that nonetheless echo, are all my very own and when she whispers about the Tinkerman, when she says "The Tinkerman is on his way to put manners on you!" – I know that she is not referring to me, or to any other real flesh-and-blood man, but rather to an ideal, as her silence dances in the nearby darkness.

HUMAN RESOURCES

When I look out of my glass cube – they joke that I am held like a serial killer – what I see are their mouths: the opening and closing mouths. Mouths relentlessly jabbering into head-sets. Mouths trying to convince, to cajole members of the general public into relinquishing their precious bank accounts details. Mouths spouting the terms and conditions on new policies. All the mouths move but I hear no sound. Not a single peep. My glass cube is perfectly insulated to ensure that everything happening inside here remains private. As acting head of the HR department, I assured Anna on this point when she came to me prior to the unsavoury incident. Everything she spoke with me about would be treated in the strictest confidence.

And here I am spilling my guts.

You see the problem was that she had begun to think of herself as being her own boss; free to come and go as she pleased, answerable to no-one. This attitude allowed her to be late most mornings, slovenly in both her personal appearance and her output at work, and downright un-manageable (according to her line manager) most of the time. And while I would never go so far as to completely absolve her of blame, I also believe the company must take some of the responsibility for allowing the situation to develop and blossom into something of an open sore. Or maybe open sewer would be more apt because her colleagues noticed this behaviour go unpunished and naturally they wondered why.

Her evenings were spent lying on the couch, drinking wine, watching television, eating ready-made meals. Life was not something she gave much thought to – rather something she shuffled around in, from day to day, with a vaguely justified sense of indifference. If she didn't care, then why should anyone else? Besides, she had a small fluffy spaniel named Yoyo who loved her, unconditionally, occupying every morsel of her free time, whose inane chirpiness kept her distracted from any sense of self-reflection. If she'd come to me sooner then maybe, just maybe I could have helped – but of course there are some people who can't be helped – no matter what you say or do for them, no matter what sound advice you offer – they simply insist on sleepwalking deeper and deeper into their nightmare.

I am in no way condoning what she did. I just think we should *understand* before we rush to judge. So far as I was aware at the time, everyone in the office liked her; gave her a wink or a nod or a silent hello, when they passed her in the corridor, or in the lunch room, with the notable exception of a blonde-haired woman, Rebecca from Purchasing. She disliked Anna and had made it tacitly obvious – though honestly Anna couldn't put her finger on a single reason why. Rather than confront the issue and discover the underlying cause, Anna chose to ignore, to allow it fester to such an extent that they could not bear to look at each other. What started as dislike slowly developed over the years into a dull, yet undeclared sourness between them.

What made it so uncomfortable was their proximity: their desks were right next to each other. The sourness, Anna had always assumed was essentially malice free, solely between the two of them and involving nobody else, a private matter if you like. In this regard Anna was grossly mistaken. The discovery of her error was made by chance one Thursday afternoon as she searched through the stacks at the back of the archive room for a missing file. Somebody must have taken it but failed to check it out on the system. Which was mildly annoying. Nothing that a trite email addressed to everyone wouldn't solve. Meanwhile some of her colleagues had come into the archive room. Assuming it was empty, they exchanged opinions on a variety of topics.

"So, what have you heard?" Rebecca murmured in her bunged-up, distinctly-nasal voice. "Possible closure. Definitely redundancies." came a confident female reply. Anna then recognised the high-pitched gurgle of that balding goon from Legal & Finance: "Good. Get rid of some of the deadwood from this place." "Like Anna you mean," gushed Rebecca, followed up by "I mean the way she leans over her screen, it's like she's looking at child porn or something." A tense snigger from all assembled. "Well, maybe she is!" from a voice that Anna didn't recognise, a voice relishing the impact of the statement on its fellow conspirators; they had all started laughing, uncontrollably, like it was the funniest thing they'd ever heard in their lives.

Like a pack of hyenas tearing a corpse apart – and she was the bloated corpse they were eviscerating. With heart clamouring, face flushing repeatedly like a broken cistern, Anna stared at her puny fists: they were turning perfectly porcelain white while trembling with anger. Her colleagues were still trying to come up with something to top the last statement. They stood around in an awkward silence, each one imagining it would suddenly materialize if they only just hung-on for another second or two. "I better be getting back!" said one voice at which point they all quickly followed suit and were sucked out of the archive room. Anna felt unbearably itchy all over her body and short of breathable air – as if they had taken it all with them. Stumbling from the archive room she slumped down at her desk in a state of numb, dumb-founded shock.

After work she returned home and stretched out on the couch. She felt incapable of doing anything. Her evening passed with the gradual lowering of light in the room. Yoyo yapped and nipped at her fingers but elicited no response from a master turned to stone. Statuesque, open-eyed, yet comatose – she nestled within the comforting softness of the cushions and was confronted by the terrifying image of a grossly overweight, misguided fool. Her only action of the evening was to shepherd

Yoyo out into the back garden where his barking was muted by the double-glazing. She then went back inside her cocoon of shame, staying there, open-eyed, for the rest of that night.

She came-to the following morning, still stuck-fast to the couch, her alarm ringing, telling her in no uncertain terms to get up. A little later than usual, she tried to compose the elements of a lunch; a ham and cheese sandwich; an apple; a handful of fun-size chocolate bars and two cans of coke thrown into her lunch-box. With no appreciation of what was happening in the world around her, in her physical sphere – she got into her car and drove on auto-pilot to her work-place. When she got there she did not leave the comfort of the car-park. Instead she sat and listened to the engine fan ticking as she gazed through the fly-encrusted windshield at that grey office building full of back-stabbing trolls and two-faced smiling haters.

Sitting at her desk in something of a trance, she tried to do some work. It wasn't possible. The proximity of the ringleader was too troubling for her. Instead she stared at her computer screen and tapped meaningless words onto it. The noise of all those voices. The awful fake bonhomie. The cajoling. All lies. All stupid bloody lies. What was the point of it all? The whole stupid game. It made her want to puke. Those meaningless words worked themselves, eventually, into a long rambling letter of resignation while the air conditioning unit above her head performed the original soundtrack over an unusual, almost dense silence in the office, with just her keyboard's keys clacking in the void.

Around eleven-ish the explanation for the silence became apparent. A spectacled girl from logistics perched herself on the edge of Rebecca's desk. They talked in whispers about the night before. Anna was able to glean much from their whispered conversation. Apparently there had been a company sponsored night out. A free-bar with a barbecue and then music. Everyone was hung-over and coming in a little later than usual. This was news to her. Nobody had bothered to invite her to join in the fun. Not that she would have gone anywhere near a place filled with such cruel vipers but it proved how little they thought of her contribution, how little they cared about her.

"Did you see the state of Steve?" said the girl in logistics. "See him? Jesus I thought I'd never get away from him," replied Rebecca. "Spill, what happened?" "Oh stop, he could hardly stand-up, he starts telling me how I'm so easy to talk to, and he comes really close up to me…" The other one tittered uncontrollably with her hand over her mouth. "I said Steve you need to sit down – you're all over the place and do you know what he said to me?" Her voice lowered but was still audible over the sound of the photocopier; "I will if you come and sit on my…" Unable to tolerate any more of this tittle-tattle Anna cleared her throat noisily. Their voices trailed away to inaudible mumbling. The rest of the day passed without incident. At quitting time, Anna placed her resignation letter in the internal post and walked quickly out of the building.

For the second evening in a row, she lay on the couch with her eyes staring up at the ceiling. Outside she could hear the cries of kids playing football and the thud of the ball against a garage door. She could hear the goal celebrations; the unselfconscious roar of a young boy celebrating joyously as he imagined the significance of his goal at a game ringed by thousands of cheering, faceless fans. Anna replayed the whole scene in the archive room again. Over and over. Every micro-second stopped, paused, re-started; and came to her senses still on the couch, gesturing wildly, shouting at the top of her lungs, at phantom work colleagues. Then an unconnected thought – where was Yoyo? She immediately sat bolt upright and then lunged out of her torpor. No, really where was Yoyo? Outside, that's right – he was sitting out in the garden. Still sitting outside, with a sad little tilt to his cute head.

Anna rushed out through the open doors to the garden. It wasn't much of a garden. An old bath-tub stuck in a pile of gravel on one side, at an angle that suggested it had been dropped, from a great height. It dominated the space of nettles and weeds around it. She expected him to bark and run at her but no; no she already knew something was wrong because it was so quiet. The back gate on to the alley was open.

Yoyo was gone. Her little friend and companion was gone and it was all the fault of that bitch; that nasty blonde bitch in work. Anna went out to the alleyway but it was half-hearted; the ignored dog was long gone. There was nothing out there but a cold breeze.

She spent the remainder of her weekend going through the motions; the motions of searching for her missing dog, while knowing deep down that she would never find him. He could be anywhere in the city. So she searched everywhere and anywhere in the immediate vicinity of her house. Every nearby lane-way, every close-by alley, stepping over a junkie here, and a homeless man there, always with the name of her dog Yoyo, trapped like a whisper behind her teeth. The pounds in the city had nothing to report. He was chipped. If he did turn up at the pound then they would contact her. What were the chances of that? They couldn't say. But surely they must have some idea? They did not. Either they honestly did not or were afraid of dashing her hopes with an honest answer.

On Monday morning, bright and early, she was summoned to speak with Human Resources. I smiled wanly when she entered, asked her to take a seat. "So you're leaving us!" I said; at which point she broke down in tears and told me everything. Having listened to her story I was troubled by one major sticking point. Yes, we could go down the grievance route, even take a bullying case, but it would never stick. Had she actually identified them by sight? She had heard voices and put names to the voices. But there were voices she didn't recognize? In trying to dissuade her from resigning or from taking a grievance I concentrated on her; what had she done to bring this on herself? I told her not to be offended, but hadn't she let herself go in the last six months? Wasn't there a chance that her own behavior had in some way…?

There is a version of this story somewhere in my personnel files in which Anna donned a tracksuit and quickly turned her life around. In one sub-version her dog returned carrying self-respect and reinvigoration in his grinning gob, spurring her on to lose weight, change her life, get out and meet people, repair all the relationships which had withered through her inactivity, solving her perpetual sloth; in the other sub-version she managed all of these things more or less of her own volition and was rewarded by the return of her dog as the cherry on top of the icing: unfortunately neither of these versions were remotely near what did transpire. Believe me – I tried, repeatedly, to reach out to her. Perhaps I did over-step the mark when explaining my theory to her – that her dramatic weight gain was a psychological mechanism for taking control in a workplace environment where she no longer felt she had any control or power over her own fate.

A month elapsed. She was sleeping fitfully. Yoyo was gone, practically forgotten. Then came the expected-unexpected news at work. She was called into a conference room with a dozen or so others: it didn't look good. Overheads were rising. Sales figures were down. And the industry was struggling to come to terms with international market trepidation. There would have to be changes made in the organisation. This phrase "changes in the organisation" caused a ripple of silent panic to course through all present. Trembling in anticipation, they were subjected to a series of slides on restructuring: what it really meant, for them. Redundancies would begin as a matter of urgency. The writing, as far as Anna was concerned, was on the wall: projected, onto a torn projector screen, in an otherwise gloomy room.

On a side-note, I announced to all those assembled that Anna's nemesis, Rebecca – would be taking over as interim Lead Investigation Supervisor. The majority of people applauded and grinned at each other. Rebecca smiled and nodded her head to accept the favourable response. Anna clapped her hands together so softly and slowly that they made no sound whatsoever. Driving home from work she stopped at a hardware store to pick up the ingredients she needed. It was so long since she'd baked anything that she struggled to find all her implements; mixing bowl, mixer, weighing scales...if she had only talked this through with me – if she could only have faced the underlying cause of her problems. But no – she had decided to go down another route.

In work the following morning, Rebecca was greeted by the sight of balloons rising from the back of her chair and an enormous card on her desk that exclaimed "Congratulations!" with an illustration underneath of a champagne bottle tilting, its cork caught in the act of popping, champagne spurting out of the open hole and two flute glasses tipping into each other in a ghostly toast. The card was slightly ajar so that she could see a whole page of signatures and congratulatory messages. Minutes later the girl from logistics appeared and made a big fuss over the card being left on the desk. In an out-of-breath manner, she rescued it, and having slid it with considerable difficulty inside a gigantic pink envelope, she tottered away out of sight.

Around three in the afternoon a little mob gathered around Rebecca's desk. She squealed in feigned surprise as they circled her, giggling and whispering, with their hands over their mouths, presumably to stop Anna from hearing what they were saying. A cake appeared, as did plastic plates and plastic forks to accompanying shrieks of congratulation. Did they offer Anna a piece of cake – they did not! But her attention was not on the cake or the giggling but on that gigantic pink envelope. Rebecca needed help to slit the envelope and slip out the huge card. Opening it out like a menu she smiled and laughed at the goodwill wishes scrawled over the insides. They stood reading the card over her shoulder, helping each other to decipher the individual words in the different styles of hand-writing. It was a petite black-bobbed woman who was first to understand; she spat her cake onto the desk and her mouth hung open so as to reveal her numerous silver fillings as she deciphered Anna's message.

All in all, five of Anna's colleagues were hospitalized, but I'm happy to report that each one made a complete recovery. As for her, I'm delighted to say that she is in a much better place both emotionally and mentally and is retraining in the area of Web Design, through an online university course connected to the facility where she is serving her sixteen months. Probationary period all clean and good behaviour will have her out before then. Naturally, medication keeps her in a stable place. Rebecca still suffers from an eating disorder that she refuses to acknowledge as having anything to do with the poisoning incident. I've tried to help her talk through this problem; to come to terms with it — thus far she has spurned each and every one of my valiant attempts.

And before you ask, no — I don't know what happened to the dog.

ALTAR BOY

For a time I was their only altar boy. My impressions include but are not limited to: shards of feedback from faulty speakers; hissing speech impediments; disgruntled rising, then kneeling, then standing, then kneeling again – as one singular sighing entity (always to the accompaniment of some screaming toddler); first-reading from the book of stumbling-mumbling-mispronunciation; inner count-down to the ringing of the consecration bells; wicker collection baskets of coppery coins and slender envelopes; the itching impatience as the priest dithers over obscure items from the two-sided parish bulletin; and always and forever – the ache of my developing knee-caps.

Under the tutelage and constant nit-picking of an old-maid sacristan Ms. Fanning, a creature never seen without her fully buttoned-up anorak, and PP Father Michael, of whom I will have plenty to say later on – I developed from an early age a virulent strain of anathema for every excruciating second, spent in the celebration of mass, and for churches, chapels, synagogues, mosques, temples – so that even now, twenty-three years later, the smell of incense, the sight of a pipe-organ, even ringing bells of any description – bring out a nasty rash on my legs and groin region.

Because both my parents were deeply devout and infinitely fearful of causing offence I could find no way of extricating myself from the web of a vocation against which I could struggle all I wanted; so long as I understood that at the end of the day I had no say in the matter. Instead I took the poisoned chalice and drank from it with a glugging sound issuing from my throat and with the general assumption that I was some kind of goody-two-shoes; a role that I was only too willing to grab a hold of, so long as it meant keeping everyone else happy and myself miserable.

The worst aspect, by some considerable distance, were the endless "dialogues" I was forced to endure with Fr. Michael. The term was his way of describing overly intense conversations in his idling car, in the listening cavernous sacristy, or on the various religious retreats to mildewed sea-side bungalows that I was coerced into attending with other fine, respectful, mild-mannered boys; retreats where the sheer tedium of his attempted brainwash and a set-up designed to isolate boys of my age – to convince them of the value of a vocation to the priesthood – failed dismally to generate any other response than shrugs of teenage shoulders.

What I am reflecting upon is the heavy burden placed on those thin, under-developed shoulders by virtue of the fact that Fr. Michael had no friends, family, or indeed, anybody else to talk to, in the way he could talk to me, i.e. a sullen twelve-year-old boy. He meant this as a compliment, I think. We had, what he liked to refer to as, a very special relationship, which meant when he clicked his fingers I was expected to drop everything: desert the classroom in the middle of a test; abandon the football match on the cusp of scoring a goal; worst of all rise from the loveliest of warm beds on the bleakest of mornings to assist in the celebration of seven o'clock mass to a handful of die-hard ingrates.

I readily admit that part of the problem was my own personality; I was regarded as a good listener, by virtue of the fact that I didn't have very much to say for myself, because I was quiet and reserved, and because I listened. The role of being a good listener I acknowledged with a bland insouciance; nodding my head in the meaningful way, frowning politely, simulating genuine engagement – on an as-required basis; I mastered all this at a remarkably tender age because for some un-godly reason people always sought me out to tell me their personal problems, cry on my shoulder, and then burden me with their unhappiness.

I didn't care. I didn't want to know. But word got out that I was a sensitive kind of a lad, someone to be trusted with a secret, someone you could rely on say in a crisis situation, someone who cared deeply about the plight of other people – they could not have been more wrong – I didn't give a flying-you-know-what about their perennial problems; but there was nothing I could do to convince anyone that I was really just the same as them in every way; just as spiteful I mean, just as un-em-pathetic, just as willing to believe the worst in other people; a real little shit actually, and a talented liar to boot. Oh yes, how I loved to lie – for lying's sake – to my friends, to my parents, to the teachers in school.

When I read in this morning's paper about Fr. Michael's passing away at the age of seventy-two, the toast spilled out of my mouth. For the last ten years he was confined almost exclusively to a wheelchair, having suffered a series of catastrophic strokes. Survived by just one sister. Nursing home for priests. A brief run-down of his years spent in the many parishes. Including this one. There is a tiny pixelated photograph of a face twisted up into a pained grimace. The tremble is still there – after all these years; years that had buried his self-important voice under a thousand tonnes of other stinking household waste.

Unwanted memories come crawling like earthworms through the mulch. I remember that day he collapsed on the altar: can still perfectly capture his rapid descent from my kneeling, open-mouthed attitude. In delivering his thoughts, on how God had a plan worked-out for each and every single one of our individual lives, he seemed to go mute – so that after a bout of flinty coughing and the dabbing of his forehead with a little cloth (the one he should have used later to wipe his mouth) there reigned supreme an infinite silence. Nervous coughing from the congregation along with worried looks all round. He stopped, stared at the bible hovering in front of him, then he danced one, two, three steps away from the lectern, very pale, very shaky on his feet – and without further ado face-planted onto the hard marble, bringing a huge gold-plated candelabra and an impressive flower display down with him in the monumentally loud crash.

A shocking scream from the skeletal Prayers of the Faithful reader brought a doctor tripping up to the altar, but only after a long wait; it seemed that time, having assumed the viscosity of lard, was intent on keeping each and every one of us prisoner of the moment. How did she even get up to the altar? Past that little gateway. I don't know. One minute just his prone body and the next she was kneeling down beside him. "Get some water, quick, like a good lad," she said. Then, after a pause the doctor whispered it to me again. I must have been in shock – I couldn't get my legs to move. It took her roaring at me for a third time to snap out of it; then I scuffled into the sacristy, still with my hands joined in prayer. Ms. Fanning was in there, doing what exactly, I don't know – her back arching upwards, rising on tiptoe, like a discomfited cat. In a gasping voice, full of dramatic conveyance, I told her the priest had collapsed, was possibly dying on the altar, needed water and in the very same breath asked if I could go home. She was too frazzled to decide. No. Yes. Go on ahead. If it would get me out of her way – she was thinking out loud, they were dull thoughts: Yes, she supposed, I could go. Before she could change her mind again, I got the hell out of there as quickly as possible.

It was the one and only time I got to leave early; the one and only time I was able to jump on my bike and make it back in time for the start of training. Is it any wonder I couldn't get on the team! Is it any wonder I was consigned to the substitute's bench – not that there was an actual bench – I was expected to sit on my hands on the wet grass along the side-line, wait for someone to get injured, then start skipping and jumping in a rigorous warm-up routine. Except nobody ever got injured.

A couple of nights after his collapse, Fr. Michael showed up to my house where my parents made a holy show of themselves by falling over every item of furniture as he came crawling inside. The doorbell ringing at that hour was enough of a surprise; "Who could that be?" wondered daddy. "The Priest!" They kept backing away, needlessly backing away, until I was forced to lower the television volume and acknowledge him; that already over-sized head now mummified in an over-abundance of wrap-around bandage. He wanted a quick dialogue with me – if that was ok with my parents – they acquiesced into a puddle and drained out of the room to make tea and pull all untidiness with them as part of this unannounced but honoured guest's visit.

It was the sheer incongruity of his presence in our sitting room made my cheeks bloom. I could feel it happening. This was truly incongruous because as far as I was concerned the church grounds were his territory and I was fully aware of my responsibilities there, fully aware of the need to comport myself in a respectful and professional way, but now he was here in my home: this was where I lived. He had completely invaded my personal space. I picked up my mother's romance novel off the floor as a means of defending myself and began reading a rowdy mis-adventure with some handsome devil and demure young woman as Fr. Michael tried to engage me in small-talk.

"That's a very interesting-looking book you're reading," he said.

With a carefully exaggerated sense of outrage I flung it to the ground so that he could have my full undivided attention while knowing that I didn't want to give it to him. At first I thought he was drunk. There was a smell of it off his breath, but he wasn't drunk. He was just emotional. It escaped in big gulps of air and sounded like a backwards hiccup, only much louder, much more pathetic. I hissed at him to keep it down. The door into the kitchen was ajar; they could hear everything. He tried to be quiet but in a portentous "see how well I'm carrying this off" attitude that left me with no other option than to scold him furiously.

It descended into whispers. There was something he needed to tell me. It was important. He wanted to be honest with me. Somehow this visit was related to his collapse up on the altar. He didn't say as much – didn't need to. I could add things up, even then. A single tear trickled, dropped from a craggy cheek, bounced off a cushion into oblivion while his wet misshapen lower lip quivered. A hand began to creep towards me; tentatively hoping to grasp something of mine, either a hand or a knee; yes he wanted to have another of our dialogues all right. Helpless, hapless, defenceless. To share a portion of his shame. The body of Christ; that was the real purpose of his visit.

His aborted confession, my embarrassed coughing, the shuffling of my feet to avoid the flabby tarantula, and then a short silent weeping fit that somehow made him feel better – before the rattle of crockery alerted us to my parents returning with the tray of swaying tidal tea in china cups and the sugar bowl and an avalanche of biscuits next to great lumps of chocolate cake (where had they hidden it?) on the very best quality plates that were never used unless an emergency situation such as had arisen here. He wiped away the tears, switched to the personality for which he was best known, and though he really couldn't stay long, still managed two cups of tea, an awkward conversation and four plain biscuits (chocolate didn't agree with his system). I picked up the romance novel from where I'd left off and kept going, to escape from the adult world.

If loneliness drives people to do desperate things – desperation makes them do even more desperate things (I forget who said that). Loneliness insisted that he couldn't go on the way he was: that he would rather be dead than go on living the great lie of chastity. So he borrowed church money and went on what he regarded as a well-deserved holiday. Somewhere hot. Where did I send him again? Malaysia. On his first day in shorts, still blue-legged and pink-shouldered he made the acquaintance of an older woman who happened to be looking for a summer fling. She took a shine to him. At first he declined her advances and yet neglected to tell her he was a priest. Declined her, politely but firmly whilst also secretly delighting in the idea that he could be seen as desirable. He rubbed sun tan lotion all over her naked back. She was a divorcee. I can't honestly remember what else I made-up about her – but I was desperate, absolutely desperate to put an end to my altar boy days once and for all.

The rumours were based on sexually explicit letters; letters written in a school-boy's careful handwriting on stolen fancy-paper, richly scented, pink, with a bordering of lovely flowers. But very well composed, if I say so myself, very believable I think – even if it was mostly plagiarized. Two lonely people thrust into an illicit embrace. It was fate that had brought them together. He so wanted to tell her. He really did, but then he didn't – partly because he was a coward but also because he didn't think he'd ever see her again, once the holiday had ended.

She'd secretly planned a trip for them out into the wilderness on the back of an elephant. That's right they were in Thailand, not Malaysia, what a delightful surprise, all going so well, until disaster strikes and they encounter a local Thai man who has been fatally injured on the trip and just so happens to be a Christian. Fr. Michael is propelled forward by his conscience to administer the last rites. It brings the dying man a terrific sense of peace while the object of the priest's affections realizes her lover's true identity, and runs away into the thick jungle. But then she comes back, if slowly, for explicit religious instruction, that I spared no racy detail in describing to the fullest extent of my non-existent direct experience.

I remember his last celebration of mass in our humble parish; how the dull rote replies seemed extraordinarily dull that night – despite the numbers sitting in front of him having swelled, for some ungodly reason – dull and yet magnificently angry. The usual tripping and slipping through the first reading. Nobody in the place was listening anyway. The Gospel that evening was the one about the Apostles not recognising Jesus among them after he has risen from the dead. The rumours had taken a firm hold because nobody really liked him anyway. He was regarded as one of these well-educated snobs that think themselves superior on account of their vast knowledge of painfully obscure Greek and Latin texts.

At the appointed time, I sent the baskets around for collection. It was a Saturday night, coming near Easter, so the juicy envelopes should have been in there. But on their return there were no envelopes in the baskets, only a few measly coins. It was obvious what the congregation were thinking: *this guy could very easily run away with the lot. To pay off his fancy woman.* Making a fool out of them. Yes, he was a highly educated chap; a learned man no doubt about it – but not much good with the people when they needed him. Not much of a pastoral service in the parish, not a man to go to with a problem. Liked to keep his distance, didn't he? A stand-offish, superior type of individual, a bit full of himself, like.

Their anger was truly made manifest at Communion time. Two Ministers of the Eucharist came down the aisles each with a ciborium filled with flesh – the circular papery-tasting flesh. From their stations the entire congregation took their Body of Christ with a silent Amen. All the while Fr. Michael was left standing on his own, abandoned by his flock, with not a single recipient willing to come within ten feet of him. It was an extraordinary sight. As pitiful and disgraceful a sight as it was – I suppose that as a sensitive boy I should have felt sorry for him – I didn't; and after mass I flung my alb at his feet and stormed out when he requested a quick dialogue.

My unwillingness to explain such an uncharacteristic outburst accompanied by tears and violent head-shaking meant they leapt willingly to the obvious conclusion. I was allowed to absent myself from any further altar boy duties and from then on we attended a different church on the other side of the town. It was understood that since I was a quiet and sensitive boy there was no point pressing me. And since my parents were too cowed to know the truth – the vague suggestion of improper conduct, based entirely on vicious rumours about him, floated freely around the parish; rumours perpetuated by a self-righteous sacristan who had discovered clandestine love letters.

He was eventually moved onto some other place, I forget where. It's probably in the obituary, but I'm not going to re-open the paper on his account. In any case – he's dead now; and no, I don't feel one bit bad about it.

ILL CONCEIVED

D avid unlocks the triple-locked apartment door with trembling hands. It's so dark in the hallway that he fails to notice his wife Rose, standing next to the coat-stand. Instead he turns on the hall light, wedging the package between his knees as he un-peels his coat. Still doesn't notice her. "What time do you call this?" she says with impeccable timing. David's very soul flops out of his body with fright. The package is juggled between his knees and hands – is very nearly dropped on the ground. She will not believe the day he's just had. But as he attempts to enlighten her – Rose turns her back on him and walks rapidly into the kitchen with the slap-stick sound of her heels on her medicated Scholls.

"Rose, sweetheart, honey, wait, I'm so sorry."

David stumbles after her into the kitchen. Dinner is ruined. Food everywhere. Stuck to the walls and counter-tops. Plates smashed all over the floor. Why? Because he was expected home over two hours ago. "I got you something," he says by way of a peace-offering. Then presents the package. "For me?" she declares, in mock surprise. David nods and waits for a slap, his eyes closed. Instead Rose takes the package and rubs it against her nose. After a long juicy inhalation, she puts it down and says, with big blobby tears rolling down her cheeks: "I was so worried that something might have happened to you."

David meanwhile has slumped down at the dinner table, overcome by a wave of wearied relief. As it all swirls above him – the recounting of her fears – he rests his baldy forehead on the palms of his stinking hands. Rose has a tendency to react violently to even the slightest change in their daily routine. Meanwhile the package is thrown to the floor and attacked – with her snout tearing open the paper and squealing in delight as the tasty offal slathers bloodily over her cheeks, chin and nose. The brutal savagery of her eating style is really nothing to remark upon. The grunts, the squelching, the salivating roars. Until at last the wax paper is covered in her spit, before being licked clean. Scrupulously clean.

"What's the matter David?" she says, once her face has been wiped with a rag; she comes to her husband, cradles his head against her chest. Gently playing with his ears she softly strokes every lovely lock of his dismally thinning hair. David grows ever wearier as he stares into the close-at-hand abyss. "There's a good boy, now eat your dinner, eh?" Without looking down, David picks up his spoon and ladles food from a bowl set below him. The spoon contains every kind of tablet and capsule, both hard and soft gelatin, every colour and size and shape under the sun. David brings the spoon to his mouth and chews on these with a loud continuous crunching as his wife continues to softly massage his temples.

A single tear rolls down David's cheek and falls epic-like into the bowl.

"Perhaps tonight will be the night?" says Rose coyly and it is about all he can manage to say "Yes, dear," while inside his head a great restrained scream echoes through the silent empty halls. To fend her off he tells her about his day. "They" don't ever listen to "his" opinions. "They" don't respect "his" endeavours. Rose nods sadly, sagely, serenely. Her husband is a useless piece of spineless flesh. She is only too aware of his enormous short-comings. He has not had the energy or inclination to make love to her in a very, very, long time. Which is not helpful when you are trying to conceive. They are trying to conceive. They will conceive. They must conceive.

Tonight she is no mood for a rebuttal. She has been fed. He has arrived home late from work. He has still not begun his chores. His normal dinner is all over the walls and floors. He is eating his special vitamin feed. He stinks of dried-in sweat. Her anus is massively inflated. These things are all the signs, all the inimical signs of a night of mating; waiting, lying ahead of them, on the bedspread. A night of great passion among the clean sheets and ruffled pillows. A night of congress in the dark arts. A night to finally savour the conception of new life.

And later, make no mistake, the task is completed: by a tearing of flesh; by a scream in the darkness; feverish breathing; hoarse whispers of instruction; by a brutal clawing at the skin between sweat-stinking shoulder-blades; a sudden slurping explosion; a hideous high-pitched cackle; two-muted hand-claps and a crash of thunder. Afterwards they cry for hours – as people often will – when remembering an act so degrading, so repellent, they can hardly bear to draw another breath. David cries down into the toilet bowl. Rose weeps into a phone receiver. She always rings a random number and cries on the shoulders of complete strangers when their love-making has finally been concluded for the evening.

Sleep though, is really such a great healer, I find. David and Rose sleep like two fresh stinking corpses. Side by side. They hold their hands crossed over their respective chests and stare open-eyed into the swirling depths. Sleep puts them out of their misery and resets their inner workings. All the troubles and worries of the moments before sleep are dissolved in the aggressive acid produced by their utter nihilistic exhaustion. They live for the warm embrace of sleep. Really can't say enough good things about it. Like death only on the shorter side. Their dreams are too dull to describe, which is funny when you consider how distorted and dysfunctional their married life purports to be.

Next morning. Dressed smartly in a crisp white shirt and paisley tie; David types slowly, very slowly, with just his index fingers whilst staring at his computer screen. His cubicle is nondescript and apart from a framed unflattering photo of Rose (a tusk of saliva linking upper and lower teeth) there is nothing individual about it. David stops typing and begins to fidget with the belt of his trousers. He loosens it a few notches and slowly massages his stomach. Despite this rubbing the pain increases exponentially. David tries to return to the typing but it's too much. He clutches his stomach with both hands, eyes wide as an incredible pain sears through his body. He stands-up and his trousers slide right down around his ankles.

"Somebody, anybody help me...arrrgh!"

It is about all he can manage to shuffle to the nearby toilets. He slumps on the throne and screams in agony. After much kicking and screaming he finds some relief and ceases to clench and bite at his fist. When his breathing has returned to normal David looks between his legs. What in the name of...? There is a small wrist-watch sitting at the intersection of the U-bend and the low water mark. This is very unusual for David. He is more used to imaginary health concerns. This is real. This is genuinely frightening for him. Perhaps he will die as a result. A wrist-watch has forced its way out of his body. He had just passed a wristwatch.

However, because of the industry he works in and the type of manager he has, there is still a mountain of work to be done before the Americans come on-line and Indians go off-line. They don't take excuses on the international bonds market. Trading will happen with or without you. Unless he keeps riding the bucking bronco market he will be left behind and asked to take his picture of Rose – and get lost. David does not want to disappoint anyone. He has a strong sense of attachment to his job despite the inherent contradictions. Despite the fact that they never listen to his ideas. They really ought to. David has wonderful ideas. He could change the course of history, if someone would just listen to him.

Back typing furiously at his computer the next wave of nausea strikes deeper, renders him unable to push the keys, and brings him sinking to his knees. His anguished cries eventually rouse the curiosity of a colleague. "Someone call for an ambulance," he hears from the ground and then "Did someone call for the ambulance yet?" and still later "Where is that ambulance, it's been two hours!" The carpet could do with a clean. People keep telling him to "hold on." Hold on to what? The ambulance is on its way. Everything is going to be alright. But why should they be? Until the ambulance arrives and the gloved hands lift him onto a stretcher, until then he has no right to imagine that everything is going to be alright.

David lies on his side on an operating table while in the background a masked surgeon examines his rectum. A cord has become entangled in his lower intestine. David is now aware of the fact that much of life is just reacting to the latest crisis or recovering from the last bout; it doesn't owe him anything, this could be the end. "Please doctor, my wife..." David whines as the pain scythes maliciously through his entire body. A nurse fits a tight gas mask over his nose and mouth. "She'll be here any second David, you are doing wonderfully well. Ever hear the one about the constipated mathematician?"

The Surgeon moves sideways, like a mollusc, over to a tool storage rack and takes down a pair of three-foot-long tongs wrapped in sterile plastic. He tears open the sterile plastic thus exposing the tongs to a dirty and germ filled world and exercises the tongs. Gives them a mighty freeing-up. "Not going to lie to you David. This will hurt a little." The Surgeon then disappears out of sight with the three-foot-long tongs as if to prove that he is no liar.

David's face registers so many emotions: surprise, astonishment, confusion and yes, of course, sheer agony. The door of the operating room bursts open and Rose hurries inside. She is gowned up just like the Surgeon, just like the nurses, and just like the students, all thirty-three of them, observing and sniggering. "David, I'm here – everything is going to be ok." The Surgeon turns to Rose. "You got here just in time, as I was explaining to your husband..." But Rose doesn't care about the details. She wants the thing to come out of David. The details are irrelevant. Just get it out of him, whatever the consequences might be; this is the moment they have been planning for, reading about, discussing, imagining, and copulating endlessly for.

And so as large tears roll down David's cheeks, the Surgeon gives a whoop of delight; and with the sound of an alarm clock ringing, the exhortations of the mid-wives, the threats from Rose, the kidding around of the surgeon, the epidural delivered by a tall anaesthetist, the screaming in agony of a man with a low pain threshold for whom the epidural has not taken effect, the pushing and tearing of flesh: finally, finally – the surgeon presents a small alarm clock on the end of his tongs. The clock is lowered into David's line of view. "It's beautiful," say Rose and David in complete unison.

"Oh David, you were so brave. The face. Those tiny little hands. Read the inscription." David reads the inscription on the base. "To David on the occasion of his first child." He beams upward at his surgeon with astonishment and delight but the surgeon is already writing out a prescription on a pad. He tears off the sheet and folds it in half. "What are you giving me?" David asks. "Instructions for use and a two-year warranty." David eases himself off the operating table like a man who has just had an alarm clock removed from his rectum – then collapses like a walrus. The epidural has kicked-in.

David and Rose leave the hospital later that night with their little bundle of joy wrapped in purple crepe paper, all snug in a little cardboard box. The alarm has been ringing continuously for the last hour. On the ride home David removes it from the box and shakes it fiercely to stop it from ringing but it doesn't make the slightest bit of difference. He raises it above his head as if he were about to dash it off the dashboard. "David, what are you doing?" shouts his wife, looking at him, looking back to the road, looking at him. "I don't know if I can handle this," whimpers the poor man. "Pull yourself together – we'll get through this as a team." That was Rose talking, but not facing David – keeping her eye on the road for the menacing shapes of cyclists and pedestrians. She examines the face of the clock and sees something odd. The two hands are spinning round and round in fast forward. "Let's get you home. You both need to rest," says Rose.

Thereafter David is confined to his room. He sits on the edge of the bed drinking hot broth and staring at the wall. He is deeply depressed. On account of the birthing experience. He has post-natal depression. The only way he can overcome it is to join a father and clock support group that meets every Tuesday morning at 11 a.m. sharp. It is there that he recovers his sense of purpose by talking about his experiences with complete strangers; listening to their stories of oppression and struggle; learning new techniques to cope with a difficult child; drinking coffee and making friends with the other parents. But that is later. First he must endure the horrible feeling that it wasn't worth it.

The little alarm clock will not stop ringing. It is not an entirely unpleasant sound. A little digital "dddee-dddee-dddee…" in itself is not displeasing – it's the sheer monotony that upsets them. It never stops. They take out the battery. They walk it around the room. They take it for rides around town in the car. Naturally David tries breast-feeding but the bond just isn't there and he beats himself up about that too. If he was a better father then none of this would be happening, etc. It never occurs to him or to his wife that they have a fucking clock and not a real baby. Just never enters their heads. I suppose that to them – this is normal. Right? That's the only explanation we can come up with, even if it is complete bullshit.

"There, there, David, there, there," comforts Rose as her husband twists and turns in the bed. From the baby room there is the sound of the alarm clock ringing insistently. "You stay there. I'll go and see to it." Rose takes down a package from the shelf. She tears off the brown paper and removes a jug of thick gloopy oil. All the while the alarm is still going "dddee-dddee-dddee…."

"I can't take it," screams David. "That's just silly-talk David, be a man." And she's right of course, being a woman. This is no way to be carrying on. He will be a man. So he pushes her out of the way and goes into the nursery, where he takes a pillow and tries to suffocate the alarm clock, leaning over it with his full body weight and mouthing "take that you little fuck" until his wife is forced to knock him unconscious with a lump of pig iron.

Then it's off to the bedroom: the room where the hyenas wait to laugh and then dig into the carcass of a happily married couple. David is dis-robed as he groggily recovers his senses. And so they begin to try again, for a second child. It's like the way they did it for the first one: only much more disgusting. And so they try again, by light touches to the ear-lobes, by gripping of sweaty genitalia, by shouting and swearing, by lowing at the exposed full-moon, by secretions from under-arm caverns, by victimisation games and role-playing of the highest order, by pure and simple fornication – and afterwards the tears and recriminations. The endless apologies.

Needless to say David is unconcerned at this point, still concussed he's not yet aware of the page that Rose has dog-eared in her maternity magazine; the one with a full-size grandfather clock. An alarm clock is a much smaller item to pass through the body than a grandfather clock. That goes without saying – but he doesn't get to take part in these decisions. Will he be allowed to go back to work? Will he be allowed to keep his own bank account? These are decisions that will be made for him. You know, the problem with David is that he's far too eager to please. But then they always knew he was different; his parents, I mean. They always knew David would struggle in the real world, so much so that once he was deemed old enough to be released from his holding-cell they instigated a plan; insisting that he marry his second-cousin as soon as he was capable of fathering some time.

Needless to say they were dead right.

F-UNFAIR

The accident happened in broad daylight on a straight road. I died. As did the driver and front-seat passenger of the oncoming vehicle. Or at least that's what the doctors are saying. They have periodic conversations about it. They say I can't breathe for myself. They say I have no control over my bodily functions; which would explain the thick plastic tube rammed down my throat, and the other one down below. If I was dead then what are these thoughts in aid of? Answer me that? One doctor is trying to convince the others that I should be disconnected. He makes a very convincing argument. It's for the best, he says, they've done absolutely everything they can and now they desperately need this room for an acute trauma patient who has been induced into a coma. My coma is not as impressive – seeing as I induced it all by myself.

The only sharp memories I have are from that funfair we attended. Do you remember? With your grandparents. You and your grandfather crammed into the car, driving in insane circles, you steering it into repeated head-on collisions, despite the warnings of that long-legged teenage ride attendant. Your feet weren't long enough to reach the pedals. Tears come to my eyes, not real tears obviously, as you steer and scream in one motion. You cannot help but scream. It's impossible to keep a straight face while watching: because you're both so entirely caught up in the moment; completely immersed in each vitalized instant, each spin of the steering wheel – and the constant danger of being smashed into.

I'm looking for your grandmother's stoop-shouldered stride among the other funfair attendees, but there's no sign of her. She might have offered some excuse or simple explanation before wandering off but obviously she didn't feel it was necessary. Not her style. Not her style to stand there and watch people enjoying themselves.

The interesting parallel is that near the town where I was killed there was an infamous train accident many years ago. Happened the year I was born. Eighteen people were killed and seventy injured in the crash. Strange coincidence don't you think? The train was derailed, the carriages jack-knifed, were demolished. Terrible tragedy. I suppose it sounds very morbid talking about this. I'm sorry. It's just that I'm dead, I think. It still hasn't quite caught up with me yet. I still need to be fully convinced by the arguments he's making; the arguments that the doctor is making, putting forth, explaining with infinite patience to his colleagues.

I'll never see you again. That's why I am speaking to a tiny shard of white light. Nothing else remains but that light. All else is in darkness and I don't have very far to go. Soon I will be quiet for good. No need to get upset about it. I assure you that I'm perfectly fine with everything. Don't mistake that for bravery though. I don't want to be dead. Perhaps you are here in the room, holding a vigil for me – although I can't say that I've heard any other voices than those of the doctors and nurses since the accident. I should have heard you say something by now. Unless my concept of time is all skewed. I don't know the answer to anything. I never figured out a single thing. Not one. My whole life. I doubt if I'll get the chance to figure anything out now. In this bit that remains.

The funfair though. It's a night in the middle of the summer. Not especially warm but bright at least. A miniature steam train is parked-up at its miniature station, the tracks ringing a wasteland enclosure on which the funfair has parked up for the summer. Not very many people around. The replica train is small and plastic; a very poor copy of whatever the original must have looked like – but you get the idea. That was all they were aiming at when they constructed it; an approximation rather than a replication. This is a train designed for children, a train for adults to squeeze-into by doubling-over. Toddlers comfortably fitting inside, with the other parent holding the buggy, waving to the two most important people in his/her life leaving by train and returning in less than three minutes on the miniscule journey to back where it started.

Nearby, a disconsolate woman in jingling bum-bag and with a football in her hand is half-heartedly trying to convince people to kick it through the holes of a back-drop painted with a goalkeeper diving full-length – to save the hole. The footballs are old and worn, the backdrop creased and tattered. She looks as if she hasn't had a customer all that day, or any other day. The look of boredom and dejection on her face is surely a mitigating factor. She holds the ball under her arm like the headless horseman. I want to help her out by going over and taking a shot; but the closer I get the less inclined I am to give her the coin. When she opens her mouth to speak it becomes a sharp harangue: "Hey, you there, come and take a shot to test your skill," she says as my path veers away from her frustrated figure.

To make matters worse, beside her barely disguised wooden shack (a converted garden shed), towers the impressive, relatively speaking, Meteoric Mouse rollercoaster ride. It shimmers in yellow and pink tubing. It is perhaps thirty feet tall at its highest point: tall enough to bring a shiver of excitement. In the dictionary definition of the word "jaded" where they use it in a sentence, my suggestion is: "As jaded as a fun-fair attendant." The one inside the ticket booth for the Meteoric Mouse is dozing on one arm and has a puss on his face that stretches from ear to ear. A sigh accompanies his movement; providing punters with change and a token. Nothing more than that. Everything in the fairground is tokenistic.

The Head Turner is one of those mechanical arms that swings a long line of seated participants in both the clockwise and anti-clockwise directions the way an old train arm would swing with Buster Keaton sitting up there. The thing itself is nothing unusual but the artwork around it is remarkable: in tight-fitting blue jeans and itsy t-shirts that can hardly contain bountiful breasts – forgotten-about celebrities from the eighties abound. I recognise a white skinned Tina Turner. Hardly appropriate for our younger viewers but at least they add a bit of spice to the ride, giving it that slightly dangerous edge, prompting perhaps this or that parent to wonder when it was last serviced by a properly qualified mechanic.

On waste ground between a dingy hotel and a swimming pool that ought to be condemned, the bumping cars provide the heartbeat to this funfair. Strapped in by a loose-fitting belt over the shoulder you begin to worry. A kamikaze eight-year-old girl will soon demonstrate that the strap needs to go properly around your shoulder and not your neck. The plastic token is placed into the slot and with a spark flying above your head on the trailing wire – off it takes, with a madman at the controls sending you head-first into a collision that will wipe the smile off the faces of everyone involved. Grandfather tries to steer but has his hand removed from the wheel by his grandson. Grandson cannot reach the pedals but he knows how to turn the steering wheel, thank you very much.

Again what is most apparent is that everyone is laughing, everyone is smiling. It is impossible not to grin or smile at the endless permutations of collisions and pile-ups, the surprise jolt from behind, the look of fear on those waiting for a car to hit them from the side – seeing it coming at them from a distance; anticipating a terrible shock to senses aroused by the music and random beeps and tuneful horns that seem to come from nowhere, when it comes, the feeling is one of relief. There is no more transient a feeling than when strapped into a bumping car. You expect it to end as soon as it starts. The panic of getting stuck. For instance, see that red-haired boy with a pure and malicious grin, the old woman with the look of apology every time she careens into someone else, the teenager reduced from snide to infantile.

The inane jingle warns us that the ride is coming to an end and so it does – all too quickly. We go looking for her but of course she's gone. You want a go inside that inflatable transparent ball that floats on a paddling pool filled with water. You want to bounce around inside the ball like other kids and experience the same thrill as a gerbil inside his running wheel. You have to be dragged away by the collar from it. In the arcade we give everything a try. In one video game we are both in possession of continuously firing machine guns that vibrate in our hands, also there is a car game where you slide off the road at every turn and explode into a fire-ball: both are finished in less than a minute apiece. We play Table Hockey for a while. You kick a football connected to a piece of rope at a computer screen goalkeeper. We play pool. Your grandfather attempts to hit a yellow, thinking it's the white. At the next table over a woman in tight blue denim makes eyes in my direction. A pool-hall wench. But that might well be wishful thinking on my part. Every moment is "what next?" The question that keeps coming from your lips as we pander to your every reasonable and not too expensive whim.

In the basketball I score 204 because I can practically reach over the basket and deposit the ball without very much effort. There are tokens to collect. These are exchanged at a booth having fed them into a machine which gobbles them up, for a receipt. For your 26 tokens you receive four of the smallest bags of jelly beans I have ever seen in my life. For 100 tokens you could have got a bumper sticker with a vaguely smutty remark on it or an empty tin can piggy bank. There are too many memories. Bad ones connected with dismal family holidays in places like this. A profound sense of disappointment comes to mind. But I'm happy to suppress these to concentrate on the present. Always on the present. Never mind what happened in the past.

The three of us go outside and see that the wet concrete is slowly drying after a shower we must have missed. Someone passing by blows smoke from a cigarette and it smells good. So damn good that I wish I had one too. But I've quit smoking – to prolong my life expectancy. We try her on her mobile phone but there is no answer. The old man goes one way and we go the other. She will have gone one way or the other.

The night is coming on. Crash of waves in the falling sky. Ten minutes later he calls, to let us know he's found her. They are going to head back to their hotel. We will see them again soon. Who knows when? Soon. Sometime in a not too distant future; days, weeks, months, years.

The next day we run into the sea. Just you and me. Nervous among the crashing waves, you will not come out with me at first. I have to chase you and put you up on my shoulder, carry you into the sea where you scream and when let go – race back toward the shoreline – then the long walk back up the beach with an exaggerated sulk, shoulders hunched, arms crossed, until I agree to play by your rules. Then I kick water into your face and we exchange water kicks until both our t-shirts are cold and sticking and the sun is never going to dry them out. The old man had gone to look for her, because he was worried that she might have got lost.

The loss of your net (a rusty broken neck) is badly felt when we happen upon the rock pools laid out invitingly beneath those cliffs of black stone. In the cool little pools we follow the flat fish camouflaged superbly – impossible to distinguish from the sand – poking at them with our sticks to stir up the sand. We can't catch them, too quick, so we stick instead to picking up slow-witted crabs who retract their legs, line them up together to protect their soft, white, fleshy bellies. But then it dawns on me that it must be time. Time to pack our bags. Time to say goodbye to the seaside and the funfair. Time to return you to the bosom of mother.

The long drive through villages and towns to bring you home. Not so bad when you are in the car beside me, talking, playing on your phone. But the return journey, through those same villages and towns, that's when I've to endure these continuously awful thoughts. No more than darts of a long-pointed stick. Reminders that all is not well. Is not and never shall be. I drop you home to your mother. Wave goodbye to you standing on the doorstep. A bag and coat under your arm. I reverse out of the driveway and head for home on my own for the three-and-a-half-hour journey. I'm so tired. I'll have to stop somewhere to get a coffee or else pull over and close my eyes for a few minutes. But not here. Somewhere further along.

The accident is quite impossible to describe. I was asleep for most of it. Dozed off just after that town I was telling you about earlier. Then a sudden catastrophic and incredible impact and the slicing restraint of my seat-belt. And now I'm here. On my own again. Or they have lowered their voices. Either way I can't hear them above the beep...beep... beep of my heart and the c-chug...c-chug...c-chug of the breathing apparatus and that single high-pitched whine of whatever it is that cleans out my bowels. I've never been so happy in my whole life. The awful itch is gone. That awful itch of being an unwelcome visitor. From eyes open to eyes closed. All gone. But you're too young to understand what I'm saying.

I had something I wanted to tell you. I forget now what it was about. Wait. They are murmuring. Those are definitely murmurs. The murmurs mean they are going to abandon me soon. No matter. I'm ready. Truly ready. Before I started talking about the funfair I had something important to tell you, something that would help you in life – words of wisdom, I suppose – but the bloody funfair knocked it out of my head and now I'm at a complete loss. It was good, you'll remember it word for word, probably want to write it down somewhere. It'll come back to me. In the mean time I'll keep blabbing away here for a while longer, if you don't m-

About the Author

Brian Coughlan lives in Galway, Ireland. *Wattle & daub* is his first collection of short stories.

Books from Etruscan Press

Zarathustra Must Die | Dorian Alexander
The Disappearance of Seth | Kazim Ali
Drift Ice | Jennifer Atkinson
Crow Man | Tom Bailey
Coronology | Claire Bateman
What We Ask of Flesh | Remica L. Bingham
The Greatest Jewish-American Lover in Hungarian History | Michael Blumenthal
No Hurry | Michael Blumenthal
Choir of the Wells | Bruce Bond
Cinder | Bruce Bond
The Other Sky | Bruce Bond and Aron Wiesenfeld
Peal | Bruce Bond
Poems and Their Making: A Conversation | Moderated by Philip Brady
Crave: Sojourn of a Hungry Soul | Laurie Jean Cannady
Toucans in the Arctic | Scott Coffel
Body of a Dancer | Renée E. D'Aoust
Aard-vark to Axolotl: Pictures From my Grandfather's Dictionary | Karen Donovan
Scything Grace | Sean Thomas Dougherty
Areas of Fog | Will Dowd
Romer | Robert Eastwood
Surrendering Oz | Bonnie Friedman
Nahoonkara | Peter Grandbois
The Candle: Poems of Our 20th Century Holocausts | William Heyen
The Confessions of Doc Williams & Other Poems | William Heyen
The Football Corporations | William Heyen
A Poetics of Hiroshima | William Heyen
September 11, 2001: American Writers Respond | Edited by William Heyen
Shoah Train | William Heyen
American Anger: An Evidentiary | H. L. Hix
As Easy As Lying | H. L. Hix
As Much As, If Not More Than | H. L. Hix
Chromatic | H. L. Hix
First Fire, Then Birds | H. L. Hix
God Bless | H. L. Hix
I'm Here to Learn to Dream in Your Language | H. L. Hix
Incident Light | H. L. Hix
Legible Heavens | H. L. Hix
Lines of Inquiry | H. L. Hix

Rain Inscription | H. L. Hix
Shadows of Houses | H. L. Hix
Wild and Whirling Words: A Poetic Conversation | Moderated by H. L. Hix
All the Difference | Patricia Horvath
Art Into Life | Frederick R. Karl
Free Concert: New and Selected Poems | Milton Kessler
Who's Afraid of Helen of Troy: An Essay on Love | David Lazar
Parallel Lives | Michael Lind
The Burning House | Paul Lisicky
Quick Kills | Lynn Lurie
Synergos | Roberto Manzano
The Gambler's Nephew | Jack Matthews
The Subtle Bodies | James McCorkle
An Archaeology of Yearning | Bruce Mills
Arcadia Road: A Trilogy | Thorpe Moeckel
Venison | Thorpe Moeckel
So Late, So Soon | Carol Moldaw
The Widening | Carol Moldaw
Cannot Stay: Essays on Travel | Kevin Oderman
White Vespa | Kevin Oderman
The Dog Looks Happy Upside Down | Meg Pokrass
Mr. Either/Or | Aaron Poochigian
The Shyster's Daughter | Paula Priamos
Help Wanted: Female | Sara Pritchard
American Amnesiac | Diane Raptosh
Human Directional | Diane Raptosh
Saint Joe's Passion | JD Schraffenberger
Lies Will Take You Somewhere | Sheila Schwartz
Fast Animal | Tim Seibles
One Turn Around the Sun | Tim Seibles
Rough Ground | Alix Anne Shaw
A Heaven Wrought of Iron: Poems From the Odyssey | D. M. Spitzer
American Fugue | Alexis Stamatis
The Casanova Chronicles | Myrna Stone
Luz Bones | Myrna Stone
In the Cemetery of the Orange Trees | Jeff Talarigo
The White Horse: A Colombian Journey | Diane Thiel
The Arsonist's Song Has Nothing to Do With Fire | Allison Titus
Silk Road | Daneen Wardrop
The Fugitive Self | John Wheatcroft
YOU. | Joseph P. Wood

Etruscan Press Is Proud of Support Received From

Wilkes University

Youngstown State University

The Raymond John Wean Foundation

The Ohio Arts Council

The Stephen & Jeryl Oristaglio Foundation

The Nathalie & James Andrews Foundation

The National Endowment for the Arts

The Ruth H. Beecher Foundation

The Bates-Manzano Fund

The New Mexico Community Foundation

Founded in 2001 with a generous grant from the Oristaglio Foundation, Etruscan Press is a nonprofit cooperative of poets and writers working to produce and promote books that nurture the dialogue among genres, achieve a distinctive voice, and reshape the literary and cultural histories of which we are a part.

etruscan press
www.etruscanpress.org

Etruscan Press books may be ordered from

Consortium Book Sales and Distribution
800.283.3572
www.cbsd.com

Etruscan Press is a 501(c)(3) nonprofit organization.
Contributions to Etruscan Press are tax deductible
as allowed under applicable law.
For more information, a prospectus,
or to order one of our titles,
contact us at books@etruscanpress.org.